Dear Philip

Thanks for the support!
Best wishes for 2019!

LEE HALL

2018

The Teleporter

Written by

Lee Hall

Text copyright @ March 2018

Lee Hall

All Rights Reserved by

Lee Hall

Published by SatinPublishing

This novel is a work of fiction. Names and characters are the product of the author's imagination and any resemblance to actual persons, living or dead is entirely coincidental.

ISBN-13: 978-1717151582
ISBN-10: 1717151582

Author Biography

Lee Hall is an independently published author from the UK. His previous works include 'Open Evening' and 'Darke Blood'.

Outside of writing Lee works as a technician for science in Oxfordshire. He has a keen interest for the stage and drama, along with a passion for watching immersive television.

AUTHOR LINKS:

www.leehallwriter.com

Twitter: @lhallwriter

Instagram:
https://www.instagram.com/this_is_lee_hall

Facebook:
https://www.facebook.com/lhallwriter/

https://www.facebook.com/drunkenteleport

Acknowledgement:

Knowing I have the belief of my readers is enough to make this whole thing worth it. Even if it's just a handful of people who make the effort to leave a review. Loyalty is hard to find in this world and so is friendship. It's particularly rare to see both of these things combined so when it comes to my writing, 'GB' is my go to guy, among many other wonderful supporters. Thank you.

Dedication:

Dedicated to those who constantly fight stereotype, prejudice and discrimination by proudly showing the world they are who they are, and so much more, very much like this story.

And I must salute all of those in the world of indie book publishing. Writers, editors and readers alike.

Publisher Links:

Satin Publishing:

http://www.satinpublishing.co.uk

https://twitter.com/SatinPaperbacks

https://www.facebook.com/Satinpaperbacks.com

Email: nicky.fitzmaurice@satinpaperbacks.com

Table of Contents:

Chapter 1: First Orders

You know, I really love booze. There aren't many things in this world that I like quite as much as booze, and I'm not trying to tell the greatest love story ever told here. I'm just telling you now that I like booze. Whether that's beer, wine, hard liquor, cocktails, ale, shots, double shots, triple shots, drinks in hollowed out fruit, drinks in fruit-shaped glasses, pitchers, tankards, those big yard measure things, stout for the more culturally inclined and pretty much anything else I haven't mentioned. Oh, and probably moonshine if there ever comes a situation.

This isn't how I ever imagined starting my story, but I've dabbled in the world of writing stuff before, (I blog, occasionally) and I know how to be original. I imagine if we were ever to meet, it would be in low light, some smooth jazz would be playing, you know that type of music nobody owns but is always there in shitty movies? A bar wouldn't be far away, maybe there's already a drink in my hand, scratch that; there is a drink in my hand and I've already got you and myself a top shelf shot on order.

So, imagine this. The image of a cityscape fading into view over heroic music. Our main character is standing there atop of a sky scraper, and maybe a stern but gently dramatic breeze is blowing. It is taco Tuesday after all. Sirens rush by and our hero slings into action.

That routine won't fly here. Reason one, I can't fly. Plus, as far as I know, we have no big skyscrapers here in Bay Valley, so the cityscape thing goes out the window. Also, I'm not a good enough guy to go out and interfere with the Police not doing their job either.

A lot of these 'stories' lack actual motive, but you'll find a girthy supply of it here... mostly. You know these modern day 'super 'hero' tales (both dirty words), revolving around a distinct lack in the motive department.

Let's take the fine example of our local plutonium delivery person. I wanna say guy or girl, but let's be neutral here, you'll thank me later (preferably Nobel style). It's been a hectic weekday for our plutonium delivery person and the previous order didn't even tip. We've all got their flyers hanging around somewhere, so all of us know where we can get our radioactive goodness at a super low price. Enter a couple of low level thugs. They intercept our person and take away somebody's hard earned ionising goodness. Well, who's putting in the save? Because our delivery person clearly isn't trained in any way to handle stuff like that happening to him. The one-dimensional hero turns up and does some flippy or angry crap; there may even be a cool vehicle and it's all ultra-dramatic. Me? I get the bus, or cycle if I'm not too hungover.

Point is, that last paragraph to paraphrase, is my way of telling you this isn't your standard comic book hero story, it's just a book. There are no dead parents here. Mine live upstate, one's a Bank Manager and the other an elementary School Teacher. My pursuit of redemption comes from somewhere else, somewhere far more ordinary.

Nobody can relate to the brooding rich dude who decides to put on a cape, or that one red haired actress who wears a leather cat suit because we all know chafing is practical. What about the middle of the roaders? I'm not talking the average guy who becomes the unsung hero, but what about the guy or girl who never needed to be a hero? They've kept their head down and paid their dues. He might even live a life with no aspirations to have rock hard abs. He enjoys dessert, but will stand up for anyone of his friends who are wronged, not just about random dessert situations like a lack of sprinkles, but in general life situations.

What about the guy who leads a steady, risk free life in his mid-twenties? And by that I mean mid-twentyish. Okay, there may be a half-truth there, so we'll say mid to late twenties, look - just not thirty okay? I'm over it.

What if I'm neither a good guy or a bad guy? Maybe in life there aren't bad words, bad people or bad things; maybe there's just bad choices and intentions. And I'm not saying every asshole who is an asshole can be a saint. Some people never ever have good in them, but in concept they are hard to find.

Anyway, let's move away from our cityscape, we're down in the bar and our drinks are served. Pull up a chair and let me shoot the breeze for a while, because this my story. The Teleporter. My real name is Kurt Wiseman and my shady memory takes me back to how this whole thing started; in a bar and probably where it will finish.

"You see Kurtis, you're still a young man and this is just your first rodeo. You've done what most people haven't, you've taken the first step."

I could always confide in Douglas Heaney; this older guy listens to all my woes and there's invariably room for that veteran father/mother figure in every story. A perfect role for that aging performer who maybe once wore the cape, but now deserves an Oscar. He always told me how it was and helped me to admit that I had a problem. And that's the first part of dealing with a problem, right?

"Now, for feck sake, drink your chaser," Douglas ordered. I watched him sink another whisky. He always turned more Irish when he drank, and he groaned whilst slamming down the glass.

I sat kind of slumped and let out a throaty belch. There I was, in 'The Drunk Poet's Society', a basement bar below my apartment building. A place where nobody knows your name, mainly because they don't show up. If there was a poetry scene it would be full of creative types and those pondering the written word, I know pretentious right? Now, there's just me sat opposite an older guy, originally from Boston, who used to write poetry.

"Okay, I got it." I slurred. Finally mustering up the courage, I gripped the tumbler and the ashy burning sensation hit my tongue.

"You're at the very beginning of this lad and the most important thing for you to do, right now, is move on," Douglas said. And he was right.

"I've been having some good ideas how." I half slurred. My fingers brushed towards a glass of stout.

"You see *'One Night'* was… was just my arrival man, it let the people know who I am." My head bobbed as I began to put the world to rights.

"*One Night in New York* was just perfect man. Not once did I ever track back, it was just me and a great graphic novel." I hiccupped as I finished tooting my own horn.

That's my graphic novel, in case you were asking. Two guys looking for revenge and who take on the mob in one rainy, gritty New York night. Their intentions; to collect the debts of the past. Sounds pretty cool, huh?

"Now with this next project, I'm gonna, I'm gonna…" I took a long sip of frothy stout.

"Sounds like you need more thinking juice. We should switch to beer, if we can get some fecking service in this place," Douglas barked from his slightly red face. He was up before I'd even finished my drink.

Across the empty bar he shuffled, past the many round wooden tables and stools; some of them with candles in big jars and others with those little electric lamps. Every available wall surface was taken up with either poetry verses in frames or books. I'm talking books in glass casings, books on shelves and quotes everywhere. Hell, even the enlarged front cover of my graphic novel stands on one pillar.

Guess I had better join him at the bar, it's probably my round and so I unhook my feet from the wooden legs and clumsily rose from my stool. My evident drunkenness a few sips away from completely compromising my navigational skills. It's a nice distant hazy-type feeling, except for my upper right leg which seemed to be twitching. I should probably get that checked out.

"You see, this is why nobody comes to this place. Who would ever go to a poetry bar? You gotta have folks who like poetry to begin with," Douglas pondered loudly to himself. He waved a hand over to the small stage set up in the corner, a single spotlight shining over a microphone.

"It's only 'cause of drunks like me this place is still open." He slammed the bar.

"Well, I like it, even if it is several flights of stairs below my apartment." I said, pulling out my wallet and taking out some notes.

"Put your money away, it's no good when you're out with me." Douglas' red face glared my way. He then shuffled along the bar and headed behind it.

"Besides somebody has gotta drink the stock before it goes off," he grinned, grabbing two glasses from above.

"Come on Douglas, at least let me pay for my own drinks?" My hands steadied me as I gripped the bar.

"No Kurtis. If you had a plus one, then I would think about it. That lass you were with before knew how to drink." He chuckled in that jolly half Irish way and began to pour me another drink.

"I broke up with Jordan five months ago man, and yeah, the fact she could even drink you under the table was a problem. Not to mention the whole sleeping with another guy thing the entire time we went out. So yeah, I miss Jordy too." I said.

"You can be a smart ass sometimes, you know that?" he slid the beer my way.

"And where do I get that from?"

"How are the book sales going?" he asked.

"Well… they are not currently. I had the initial buzz and the whole 'hey, you wrote a book' thing and now? It's as busy as this bar," I grumbled, triggering a wheezing laugh from Douglas.

"I've put me life savings into this dump, but I can still laugh about it. Cheers," he said, and we clanged glasses.

"Tell me about the new book? What you gotta do is move forward, get more stuff out there."

I took a big swig of fizzy goodness and composed myself. Again, the leg twitching came but it didn't stop me talking to the 'one man press conference' that was Douglas; the only guy interested in my work.

"Well, you see Douglas, I've done the whole gritty New York mob revenge story. This time around, I'm thinking comic book hero. Maybe even a duo, but instead of good guys we've got two bad guys," I said.

"Comic book heroes with the whole bad guys angle, huh? Sounds desperate to me," Douglas said, "but you follow your heart and your thoughts. I did, and it got me to this place and there were some good in between times. Life is a tree, you start at the top…

'Here we go again with Douglas' analogy of life,' I thought to myself.

"You start life atop of this grand tree and hit your knackers on every branch on the way down to the ground," I said, finishing the man's famous outlooking quote on life. My Irish accent wasn't as authentic, no matter how much stout I'd had.

"Don't forget when you finally break onto the ground a dog comes and pisses all over you," Douglas said.

"So, remember, life is all shit anyways and you gotta make your best at it, son," he added inspirationally. Well, to me anyway. And he was right, again.

It was then I decided to fully knock back the beer and go do something with my life.

"Monday means a new week, and today is Monday, so it's time for a new frickin' start," I stated with a sharp gassy belch. I stepped back and stood proud.

"Hear, hear!" Douglas said, with a delicate raise of his glass.

Just as I was about to blow out of that joint, another breeze blew in. Five or six high pitched loud voices cruised toward me and the bar.

"Another?" Douglas asked.

"Yeah, one for the road," I said and shakily grabbed a stool as the beer took effect. Curiosity held me back to see how this was gonna go down.

"Oh my god! They have like karaoke here!" One of them squealed, as they flocked towards the stage and microphone.

"It's for poetry," Douglas growled, with his no nonsense voice. I could sense the girls disappointment just as I caught sight of one of them wearing a pink sash.

Bachelorette party on a Monday night? I couldn't exactly discriminate as I gently sipped the new beer.

"But I can fire up the karaoke machine if you girls want?" Douglas called out and winked at me.

They screamed in approval as Douglas made his way to them. I faced the bar and left them to their own devices, but this was it. One drink and I'm heading back up to make another awesome graphic.

"Turk-wise! Is that you?" A high-pitched voice demanded.

I hadn't heard that name since High School and made all the more awkward as this bride-to-be was accosting me with it. Not that I had a problem with the attention, but looking at her I remembered the face and not the name. We are probably friends on that life-invading site and still I couldn't see her name next to a pair of apparent model style photos.

"Hey, you," I said half-heartedly.

"Now, I heard from somewhere that you have written a book?" The apparent model who used to go to High School with me asked.

"Yeah, it's a graphic novel, but yeah, not a big deal no." I said, only it's probably all I ever talk about.

"What about you, 'bride-to-be'? Apart from the obvious knot-tying activity, how's life been?" I added.

"Well I've been travelling and modelling..." Queue the snoring. Especially as her voice went up and down in a rolling pitch, please somebody, get me the damn mute button. Being semi-drunk allows you to skip scenes like this and so I did, she's not a principal character anyway, two scenes max. I successfully glazed over until she seemed to raise her voice to another decibel.

"Then I met this super awesome guy, so we're getting married!"

I've got an Instagram too, so does that make me a model? And that whole travelling thing, she probably went to France one summer and then got back with the asshole she went to Prom with. Why am I attacking this girl? Well folks, it's because what she said next was,

"I really want to read your book, you should totally send me one." This was followed by my usual glare of 'maybe you should pay for one yourself and help a guy out'.

It's not like I had put all my hard-earned savings into creating something I'd made from my own mind. I'm not bitter, I just don't like every conversation I have with someone I barely know turning into a pile of shit just because I'd made something creative. I'm not judging you, if 'One Night' ain't your bag, I'm cool with that, let's get drunk instead.

"Come on, Stacy, we're gonna sing Rihanna!" One of her whining tag-along's said.

Bingo, that's her name; saved by a high pitch squeak.

"Well, congratulations Stacy," I said and took another sip of beer.

"Who's your friend?" The tag-along enquired as she appeared alongside Stacy.

"This is Turk-wise, that's what everyone called him back in High School. He used to make these goofy comics and sell them. Now he's published for real," Stacy explained. To my resentment.

"No way."

"It's totally awesome. He's like a celebrity now," Stacy said.

Okay, so my approval of her went up only a tad.

"It's Kurt, and it's no big deal, really." I held out a hand for the girl to shake.

"Tara. Nice to meet you Kurt," she said and I took her soft hand. Maybe she would go out with me was the thought I had right there and then, maybe it's because I'm a sad single guy and she's girl showing me compulsory attention.

"How about I get you girls some shots and I'll let you party. I've got another book to write." I tried.

A barrage of screams blared through me and I slid off my stool.

"But you've gotta stay and have a shot, I'm getting married," Stacy demanded.

"Just one?" Tara asked and fluttered her very probably false eye lashes at me.

"Tequila?" I asked the honorary girlfriend for what was supposed to be a drink.

This 'drink' then turned into a strangling rendition of Rihanna; 2-for-1 cocktails thanks to Douglas, some Madonna and Bon Jovi, two more tequila shots and another beer. This all finished with a team effort of 'We are the champions'. Somehow, they propped me up centre stage and even though the room seemed to spin and my leg twitched again, I managed an air punch finish which was followed by the main bar lights coming back on.

"I hate to be the bearer of bad news ladies, but it's closing time," Douglas announced. He had already begun to stack stools on tables, as the team harmony of groaning disapproval came his way.

Just as quickly as the storm of high pitched screaming had come, it blew away and was out of the doors. I couldn't even remember getting a goodbye or a thanks. Right then I had my own problems, like navigation and basic functions.

"Looks like you had a good night Kurtis," Douglas smirked nearby, I couldn't really tell where as my head flopped to one side.

"The best nights always come from nowhere," he chuckled.

"Yeah," I agreed with shallow breaths.

"What have I told you about not coming here anymore?" Douglas barked in a change of tone.

"Huh?" I asked through one side of my mouth.

"You know I'm always gonna drop by 'D-man'," purred the friendly voice of a woman I knew.

Laura Owens or nicknamed 'Big L', all her own idea, made her way to the bar. This larger African American lady used to work the door here at the Drunken Poet's Society. My impaired vision caught her eye as she began to help stack the chairs on a table.

"My shift down at the harbour starts in an hour and you're on my route. Probably where the 'Daddy bought me a Mercedes' crew are headed to next," she added.

I caught sight of her looking up and out at Stacy's gang. They'd stumbled up the steep concrete steps. Even steeper the drunker you got, trust me.

"How much did they drink? Oh crap, Kurt is here, so they're gonna be a pain in my fat ass."

"Hey, Big L," I said over another burp. "Your ass isn't fat, it's great. I'm gonna need your help, again." I held out both arms like a kid ready for bed.

"Again? Damn, can't you cut this guy off, D-man?" Laura asked.

"He's me only customer and it started off as a few quiet drinks. But tonight, I've got takings. Now get outta here before I pay you," Douglas said.

"I guess we're doing this again. That's only coz I haven't worked my legs this week yet."

She scooped me up in her big arms. Was this weird? To me it was the norm, here's this bouncer girl who would carry me back home when I drank too much.

"See ya later Douglas," I cheered over Laura's shoulder.

"Damn you're smelling fine girl," I added and rested my head on her.

"Full of compliments tonight, aren't we? Let me guess tequila?" Laura asked.

We moved to the door.

"You know me so well." I grinned back at her. "Where would I be without the Big L? Big L by name and Big L by nature. You're the LBGT saint of a character in my somewhat boring life story." The breeze of outside hit me and I lurched slightly before burping loudly.

"You gonna chuck, you gonna chuck?" Laura demanded as she held me forward like a puking kid.

"I'm good, I'm good, it's just the fresh air," I mumbled and settled back.

We moved up the first steps towards the street.

"These are my best threads son. You don't wanna be puking all over them."

"Security guard is totally your colour Laura, and that's not a race thing that's just fact..."

"Do I need to drop your ass again Kurt?"

"No, no, not this early in our journey. Maybe onto that trash pile if you have to, but please don't," I begged.

Everything spun around as we moved into the main apartment building.

"And keep the noise down, most normal people are sleeping at this time on a Monday, Jesus."

"You have to understand Laura, most of my neighbours, they are assholes. Especially that bitch opposite me. Damn it my leg is twitching again. If I stretch out it goes away." I awkwardly spread myself out as Laura tried to carry me up the apartment block stairs.

"You gonna answer that?"

"Huh?" I asked.

"The vibrating in your damn leg Kurt, it's your cell phone, someone's calling you."

"Oh yeah, so that's what it is." I closed one eye to get a better view at my cell's glowing screen, as I went to answer the call it ended and then I read it.

"Five missed calls? What the actual shit? Shit, shit, shit, shit in a s sandwich, shit on a stick," I swore.

I was moving into that drunken over talking phase, even though I could hardly hold my head up.

"It's Jordy, she's tried to call me twelve thousand times."

"Didn't you guys break up like five months ago. Screw her man," Laura said, and we hit another floor.

"Yeah, that's the one thing I didn't do."

"I know because I carried you that night as well. You mainlined red wine if I recall, then we watched DVDs on wrestling until dawn."

"You see that's why your perfect for me," I grinned, playing up to the joke crush that I had on the probably only reliable safe person I knew.

"My grip suddenly feels loose," she threatened good humouredly.

"We've watched cage matches together! Please don't betray me," I begged.

Without even getting out of breath she carried me up to my floor. Just when I was about to slip out of consciousness, she spoke;

"Looks like you got a visitor Kurt."

"Huh, I'm here?" I asked and my vision angled down to a swathe of red covering the floor.

"Somebody spill something down here?"

"Nah, son, they were put here intentionally. Rose petals and they're leading right into your half-open apartment door," Laura said.

"I really should change my locks or even better, actually try using them."

"Want me to go in first. Secure the area?"

"Nah, Big L, we can handle it. To the apartment!" I shouted and raised a charging finger.

We moved all two steps and Laura pushed the door.

"I've been waiting for you," came a soft voice. My almost stroke-like condition didn't allow me to look straight forward. Okay, maybe stroke is an overstatement, especially if you're a stroke patient, however I had lost most of my functions right about then.

My eyes staggered along the wooden floor of the apartment and up to some bare legs. Who's this I thought? With all hopes forward, maybe Stacy had brought the party upstairs. Continuing to look up, I saw a relatively decent pair of knees and then the snake! The snake tattoo, 'no! Oh god no'.

"Jordy," I cried out in a semi-conscious slur.

"Didn't you guys break up five months ago? Damn." Laura shook her head.

Jordy stood there in just a zip-up sweater; my hooded zip-up sweater!

"I want you back Kurt, so I let myself in," she said so innocently. Don't let that fool you. The snake is the real deal in terms of her personality.

"And I found your turquoise sweater. It's so comfy and I thought you wouldn't mind."

"Oh, he minds. You weren't here for ground zero girl. We watched wrestling until sunrise," Laura added.

"Oh, maybe I made a mistake. I see you're with Lauren now then, I thought you were..."

"It's Laura! And yeah, you thought that right..."

"No, no, no. It's not like that, she's... and I'm... well, we're not together. Okay?" I growled, probably at the wrong person and she let me drop to the hard floor.

"Laura?" I moaned in pain. "Big L, come on girl, I didn't mean it like that," I cried.

"What about the cage matches?" I called, as Laura slammed the door shut behind her.

My winded body tried to turn towards the girl in only my turquoise sweater.

"Come to bed Kurtis, I promise I will make it worth your while," she said, blowing me a cliché kiss.

"I'm… already… there!" I groaned, doing my best to drag my numb body towards the glass bedroom doors. 'Come on Wiseman, pull'.

"Please wait." My hand reached out. God, I was so drunk.

"Have you been drinking again?" she asked in an immediate change of tone.

"Huh? What made you think that?" I rolled over on the floor and crashed into my armchair. Somehow, I managed to prop myself up against it. There I sat, slumped at an angle which would ache for a week, and then I tried to talk.

"Look, Jordy. We had a thing, but that's all it was, just a thing, and that was a 'was', not an 'is'," I slurred. "I knew you were sleeping with that dude the whole time man. Not cool, not cool man."

"I've changed Kurt, he made me realise how lucky I really was." Jordy pleaded.

"Why? Could he drink more than you?" I laughed.

"What is that supposed to mean? I came here tonight, I even tried to call you."

"Well I ain't hard to find," I argued and couldn't keep my eyes open anymore.

"You know what? Fine then. If you don't want me, I was with someone else anyway." Jordy said and that was the last thing I consciously heard her say.

"Uh huh, that's great, just leave me my sweater before you go..." And like that, I was no longer for this world, but rushing head long into a weird dream land which seemed to make my head ache more and more.

Chapter 2: Second Round

I really hate booze and let me tell you; there aren't many things I hate more in this world than what that poison does to you. What's more, let us not overlook the comparable contrast of how the last round opened, that's literature for you. The glinting sunlight bruised my aching existence the next morning and I knew I'd moved into the remorseful phase. I groaned, not in pain of the headache, but from the holy hell of what happened last night. The snake girl burned into my mind.

That witch had even found my prized turquoise sweater and used it to encase her dirty cheating body. I really hoped she hadn't taken it and then my answer came. My pained neck and head brushed over the soft familiar material and momentarily I opened one dry eye. She had probably tried to throw it in my face on the way out and now most of the turquoise fabric had become my pillow. I plumped the makeshift head rest and rolled over on my flat wooden floor bed. If I lay still, the pain and dizziness might go away.

I winced yet again as I recalled how I'd spoken to Laura last night. Remorseful embarrassment does that to you, sometimes. Then my mind tried to drift past the drunken events I'd gotten myself in.

"I dunno Lou, he looks shot to pieces." The peaceful silence was broken by a man's Brooklyn accent.

"I doubt he's got any more talk in him."

"All that liquor didn't just make him talk Vinny, he sang. Pissed that big broad off in the process. Let's face it kid, we've got no hope with him like this," muttered another guy, his voice deeper than the first and he seemed older.

"Huh?" I opened the one eye again.

With blurry vision, I saw two shady figures standing over me. One of them with a smoking cigarette, the other taller with a trilby hat on his head.

"He's thinking of doing 'super heroes' next. No chance of a sequel for us anytime soon then," Vinny said. His high-pitched buzzing voice bothering me.

"Guess it will always be One Night for us," Lou said.

"Go away," I groaned and attempted to roll over.

"You're the boss, Boss," the deep voice of Lou added.

"Yeah, we was just remindin' you of last night's conquests, mainly pissing off the Big L."

"I didn't mean to," I groaned, my fingers pressing over the pride badge on the inside of my zip-up.

"You know, guys like you need to be wearing that badge on the outside if you want it to count." I could almost feel Vinny's judging frown.

"Why are you here?" I growled.

"Somebody's gotta act as your alarm clock. And you created us, remember?"

The fellas from New York shuffled over to my big writing desk, the place where they were made. Sweet silence then ruled again as I blocked out the conscience made up of those two debt collectors.

"Alarm clock," I chuckled, it was then a wounding realisation hit me. It was morning!

Every internal muscle lurched me up and forward from the torture rack that was my painful floor bed. The time; 8.15am. I should have got up half an hour ago. Guess I was gonna be late, screw it, I'll think of something on the way.

The bass of shouting reverberated through my walls from the hall, whilst I headed to the bathroom.

"Fine, then go! And don't come back!" The bitch opposite me shouted. It was her usual running gag of breaking up with her equally asshole boyfriend who owned an abusively loud car.

He yelled something back before a loud crash resonated across my floor.

"Domestic abuse? Our subjects are evolving," I noted out loud and twisted the shower dial.

The rush of hot water did nothing to numb the ache, and I laughed at how those bachelorette party girls dragged me up on the stage to sing last night.

"2-for-1 cocktails," I chuckled to myself before moving on to drying. For a second, I caught a glimpse of myself in the half-steamed mirror. Looking back at me was the fine figure I had become. A solid two-pack sat below a sad set of pecks. I poked the bags underneath each eye and convinced myself that there was no time to worry about my ticking body clock. Not that I was trying for kids any time soon.

"Late, late, late... latte?" I asked myself. Maybe I had the time for a vanilla latte on the way to my bus stop.

Clothes on? Check. Phone, wallet and keys? Check. Turquoise hoody up? Check. Dignity? Down in the bar, lost three years ago along with most of my savings. I grabbed my rucksack and headed out the door.

The creak of floorboards opposite me stirred me into action and I flung the door open, feeling immediately exposed. My hands worked at putting the key into my lock; that should keep the Jordy-type snake girls out.

Another feeling of frowning eyes burned through my hood, this time from a real person not one from my conscious. She was standing there, that bitch from opposite.

"Morning," I croaked and kept my head firmly down. Avoid eye contact, I mean who likes their neighbours anyway?

"Hey, looks like somebody picked a fight with a florist out here last night," she snarled.

My eyes caught sight of blonde hair and a pencil skirt. I looked down at the rose petals left by Jordy.

"You know anything about this mess?" The bitch demanded.

"Nope. Well, have a good day," I said and coursed away with her eyes following me.

"My boyfriend slipped on them. My ex-boyfriend, I mean. Asshole. He deserved it."

There came the kind of silence that only follows conversation killing words. I stopped, which made it worse.

"Anyway, see ya soon Kurt."

"Cool." I added and made for the stairs.

Why did I call this girl the bitch across the hall? No reason. In fact I didn't even know her, only that occasionally she would flip out and go full-on marital with the guy she was seeing. From that I thought she was a bitch and considering she lived across the hall, I just merged those concepts. Some things are what they are.

Now why am I mentioning the bitch across the hall? Well friends, she just may happen to be a somewhat relevant character in this little word party that we got going on here. I'll ask the questions here and answer them later during the important plot points, that's called resolve. You can have that lesson for free, or for however much you paid to read these words.

There's no way to make a hungover Tuesday morning bus commute across Bay Valley interesting. So, I won't mention it further. Time stood north of 9.30am by the time I walked into the wide blacked-out glass building that was Liqui-tech. My sneakers squeaked on their shiny marble floors and even in my lateness, I chose not to take the elevator for claustrophobic reasons. I zagged to the staircase door.

I work in Brand Outreach, which probably sounds like some bullshit right? For Liqui-tech, a big-time player in science stuff. I say 'stuff' because I don't know half the crap they make or do. Maybe you're thinking I should probably know something about the company to work in 'Brand Outreach' right? Well I haven't been found out yet and let's keep that our little secret because the pay is steady, and the conditions are relaxed.

So, what is it that I do in this modern work place for seven and half hours a day? Not much, but here's the story kids; next time you find yourself sitting in the reception of some stuffy office, look out for the typical brochure that's sitting on a glass table as you wait for your job interview, or even better, those work place posters scattered around.

Just think of that typical image, the one where there's normally a suited-up guy with a smarmy smile, he may even be holding a clipboard or smiling down at a computer with some false results. Opposite him is the youngish looking broad smiling. Maybe she's leaning over him or the desk. He desperately wants to make more than small talk to her but goes home at night and cries himself to sleep, masturbates some more and crawls through life only wondering every now and then how socially inadequate he is.

She on the other hand would wish at least one guy in the office would stop checking out her ass or tits and treat her for what she can do, not what she looks like. She'll stay at the office until seven to prove that and then change into sneakers for the journey home. On the way, she'll pick up a bottle of wine, after all anything over five bucks is all the same anyway, that's what she thinks, and she'll drink it and then move onto the liquor cabinet with high hopes the booze is enough to drown out her depressing spinster life of assholes hitting on her at work.

Specific, right? You see I'm all about the detail, and that picture I painted for you is what I strive to succeed in all the Liqui-tech brochures. Putting together a picture like that, with such undertones, is half my imagination filling in the gaps and the other half tricking those two 'model' employees that they are the face of the company. I also update the website and social media stuff using my adept powers of blagging. It's a good gig with very little management interference, the only guy I work with is my manager and he's casual to say the least. As long as I coast out of his way, he coasts out of mine. I mean who in their right mind wants to work, right?

Even our office sits out of sight, at the end of a curved hall next to a cleaning supply cupboard. A single door pane looks into the poorly lit windowless hovel I'll call home for the day. This time around it's darker than usual as the lights are off. Phew, guess me being late will go unnoticed. I pull out my key and open the door.

The two fluorescent lights flicker to life as I enter my print room-type place. By the door sits Marcus' desk; empty and deserted. He'll check emails and spend the day reclining, maybe even offer to show me a YouTube video, all this to look forward to when he finally gets in. Thank the lord he wasn't there to see me shuffle my hungover ass to the desk stuffed behind a shelf unit, although he wouldn't notice or give a shit, that's real management for you. Some days we don't even talk, maybe a nod or grunt is enough. Take that personnel and your death by PowerPoint seminars about 'communication in the work place'.

"And breathe," I said, knowing that nobody else had noticed my lateness. Maybe I could even catch a couple of winks. My sneakers crossed each other up on the paper strewn desk and I leant back. Just when everything had settled, the door burst open.

Marcus Preston had made it in, late like me. His jolly frame breezed towards me and my horizontal state.

"I was late as well," I said.

I watched the guy kind of moonwalk with his shoes squeaking on the plastic floor.

"What have we got today then?" he asked and I shrugged.

"Good, that's how I like it. Hang tight kid, we may get some work this month, but I'm not holding out."

Truth is, Marcus is a good dude. He's what you call a 'lifer' in the company and has worked every position going. So, he knows his stuff. He shuffled away and back to his desk. His seat clunked as he reached full recline.

My office chair sprung forward as I reached up to grab my headphones; maybe the pounding of music will pound out the actual pounding in my head.

"Actually…"

Shit. I guess there's something he wants me to do. Again, came the squeak of moonwalking shoes and Marcus busted a move my way.

"We got an email last night. A new demo is happening downstairs. The big boss has requested social media coverage and we all know that the jokers in our marketing department can't read, write or spell." He handed me a ruffled piece of paper which had clearly been screwed up and trashed. There was even the resemblance of a penis shape drawn in thick pen.

"This is from Williams. 'The' Henry Williams," I said.

"Yep, that asshole, or at least whoever is wiping his ass these days. Well, I ain't going down there, so you better. I already filed this away, but someone better take his request seriously. Grab the camera and go down and make us look like we care. I would, but we haven't spoken since '96 and the year after that I lost all work ethic."

There's an epic back story somewhere between Marcus and the owner of Liqui-tech. We'll revisit this little subject later. Before I could delve any deeper his phone began to play the looney tunes theme.

"And that's the real boss calling. Son No2 was up all night with a temperature, so I'd better take this. I may duck out early today so if you don't see me... hey, honey..." and like that, Marcus breezed out.

With only a handful of minutes until this presentation, I dragged myself down several flights and across the reception lobby. The line of people who cared to attend this early demo were stacked and waiting to head into a big cinema style conference theatre. I joined the queue and checked the camera around my neck.

The double beep of doom meant only one thing as the display flashed.

"Low battery, shit." I said, thinking of turning back.

Brand Outreach needed a win here. Especially if we wanted to show marketing a thing or two about doing their job properly. I'm all for being lousy at my job, but there's no excuse for poor performance, that's different from being lazy. The Liqui-tech marketing department is famously poor at spelling and it grinds my gears. Right then though, I had other problems, like this assface of a camera being low on power.

"Most cell phones take camera quality photos," a voice quietly advised said me. My annoyance distracted me for a second, then I saw a set of eyes giving me a friendly stare. It felt weird and icky because whenever that stare had burned through me before, it had been ferocious.

The bitch from across the hall? What is she doing at my place of work? My private space of zen had been violated by her pencil skirt and tight-fitting waistcoat.

"Oh, hi." I said in a defeated type of surprise, "what are you doing here?"

Did she work here? That would be embarrassing. She reached into her grey waistcoat pocket and pulled out a lanyard, on her badge read 'Press'.

"Henry Williams is the most newsworthy guy in Bay Valley, Kurt," the bitch said, "and all for the wrong reasons. So, I wouldn't miss an opportunity to give an asshole like Henry Williams plenty of shit, and maybe even get a story," she whispered to me. Her eyes constantly scanning around as if the secret police were watching.

We crossed the doorway and headed down some steps to see a bunch of people spread far and wide in rows of blue seats. A wooden podium sat in a spotlight up on stage and behind that, a blue curtain stretching high and wide. For all I know King Kong could be on the other side. A distinct smell of carpet hit me, you know that plastic smell you get in lecture halls?

"The Press are down there," the bitch said, and I found myself following her.

"It's Casey by the way, regardless of what you have heard, it's not actually 'bitch across the hall'," she said, and paused for a second. Did she just use her nickname?

"Now who's been using names like that?" I asked. We were amongst people on laptops and others with cameras at the ready. Was this demo really a big deal?

Casey shot me a 'cut the bullshit' type of look and we moved into the middle of media city.

"I've read your blog Kurt," she pulled down a seat and I did the same.

Did I mention this bitch in my blog? Wait a minute, I had a blog? I cast my still aching mind back.

"I'm kidding, but I do read your stuff. It's okay I guess, just don't quit the day job yet." Casey smirked.

"Thanks, I guess."

She flipped open a notepad and began the interrogation.

"What do you know about this demo then Kurt?"

"Uh, zip." I said vacantly.

"Okay... what about Williams? You know he's a big supporter of our less than great President and he also hates the Press. Apparently, it's all fake news," Casey said, and I cast my mind back to the Presidential Election. My view fades momentarily to a rather drunk affair and Fox news.

"I can't feckin' believe it, he's only gone and got in, that feckin' walking tribble. Feck sake, shut it all down now..." Is all I pretty much remember from that night, that and Douglas Heaney being outraged. It all went downhill from there on, I'm talking Gin style.

"I wouldn't know, I would have voted for the other guy anyway, but I was busy," I said to Casey. And yes, folks there's is a political undertone to this story, but it's light, kind of like a light beer. If every other dip shit wants to express their opinion through satire, then I will too.

Casey bowed her head and smiled.

"There's a lot of Press here, geez." I said, looking around.

"Uh huh," Casey hummed in agreement and then closed her notepad.

"Where you are going?" I asked, and suddenly we were both on the move.

"Williams is famous for throwing out the Press, so I don't want to associate," Casey whispered back to me and headed up a few rows. Again, we sat down and then the lights went down.

The flash photography began as the entourage filed in through the same doors we had. Some 'large' men dressed in 'body guard' black shuffled the surrounding photographers away and in the middle of the people hurricane came a stocky hunched-over man.

Henry Williams corrected his posture and then swaggered in a way all millionaires do, like he's got more money than everyone in the room and that he doesn't give any shits. His thin silver hair flapped as the ventilation gently blew past him.

"Somebody shut that off," he commanded, as he used a wrinkled hand to batten down his possible flailing wig.

The group swarmed all the way down the stairs and yet even more members of the Press seemed to surround Williams. His large men made easy work of them and kept everyone else at bay, all so he could climb the three steps leading up onto the stage.

"Not a bad turn out," he said in that self-assured way.

"Even if there are some faces who are like a bad rash and just won't go away." The audience gently laughed at his ice breaker style, "but even my critics will want to see this." He paused and raised one finger, everyone in the room fell silent.

"Thirty years ago, a group of scientists had a vision, a vision which only someone like me could fund. A start-up called Liqui-tech was formed after some ambitious college graduates convinced me to invest in their minds. Business and science has moved on after all those years ago, but money and results are still the driving factors. Ladies and gentlemen and unfortunately the Press, Liqui-tech is proud to showcase our latest project."

Henry Williams held up both hands either side of his pinstripe suit jacket and the blue curtain behind him slid open.

Behind a darkened glass we saw a mass of glowing light. I couldn't make much else out, apart from the moving shadows at the base of what looked like two tanks of liquid standing side by side. Their colour was an almost neon or electric blue.

"For the last decade, our policy here at Liqui-tech is to aim for a zero pollutants policy, something which we have delivered with excellence…"

"That's bull," Casey whispered to me.

"All of our experimental projects have to be clean. Some would suggest this is purely an environmental issue, but it is also has financial benefits for this great nation. Behind me is what started out as a vanity project but will now convince you that Liqui-tech is at the very forefront of science in the 21st Century. You are all looking at the first ever Quantum Displacer port, built right here in Bay Valley."

"Quantum technology? Hashtag nineties." Casey scoffed.

Henry Williams talked some more, and I watched Casey take notes in the shadows of our audience seating. He said some other science crap and stuff about money, but if you ask me, I don't know what a Quantum Displacer is either. I could have nodded off as the glass backdrop began to change colour.

"To introduce and walk you through this Quantum Displacer is a friend and long-time colleague; Professor Receding Hairline and thick glasses."

Okay, so his name wasn't really that, but I couldn't remember it fully, I think it was Professor Rice. Again, I should know but I don't read those circular email updates about the company.

He appeared alongside a pair of walking white coats in the big white tiled room behind the glass. He took off a set of ski mask type goggles and normal light came up around them. The tanks now glowed in a dark purple colour. Around them I could see piping, cables and computer screens. This was the ultimate mad scientists cave.

"Thank you, Henry. We are going to demonstrate this morning how this displacer works. Now, these two separate tanks you can see are separately bonded. They are airtight, liquid tight and even electronically tight. If I were to stand inside either with a cell phone there would be no reception. Nothing can get out of either; the various cables and pipe work you see going into each tank before you have no connection to either tank whatsoever," Confirmed the Professor.

"Well, I think you've convinced me, anyway. So, both tanks are airtight and aren't connected to each other in any way?" Williams repeated the statement as a question. This turned into an apparently rehearsed charade and seemed as cheesy as hell.

"That would be correct, Henry."

"Like so many of the audience, we are dying to ask; Professor, what are the contents of these tanks? And are they toxic."

"As you are aware Henry, all of the products we create use zero pollutants, so my answer is no, the solution in these tanks is not toxic…"

"Again, that's bull," Casey said, only this time someone in front of us turned around.

"Well, what is in the solution Professor?" Williams asked.

"Not a lot in layman's terms, Henry. For this experiment we have taken water, just normal purified water and we have put that water through an even more advanced purification process. So much so that the solution in either tank will no longer conduct electricity," the Professor explained.

"So, you have simply demineralised water. Why?"

"To an extent, yes, Henry. It's the perfect blank canvas. Now let me show you." The Professor turned to his team.

One of the white coats approached with what looked like a radio with an old-time cassette player.

Classical music echoed out through the lecture hall's speakers.

"Beethoven is my personal choice," the Professor shared. He then instructed his duo and pointed upwards. They moved to a metal ladder in between the two tanks.

"Now, theory suggests if you were to drop a normal electronic appliance into standard water, the components would short out and that would be the end of it. In our solution, which we call dry water, the music will continue to play if immersed."

I sat forward and looked up. With one white coat opening a hatch, the other dropped the radio into the tank. For a second it floated before sinking to the bottom.

"As you can see there is no visible sign of distress for our music playing apparatus. But how can we know for real?"

The two science lackeys scrambled back down the ladder as Williams talked some more,

"Well, Professor, you said either tank is bonded. Nothing can get in physically."

"That's right, Henry. Whenever you are ready," the Professor said to his returning duo. They both sat down at a computer terminal.

"Now, we will display the purpose of this liquid. By exciting the contents of both tanks with the right electronic frequency, we can link them and although you can't hear Beethoven currently, I guarantee it is still playing."

From speakers behind us came the eerie echoing sounds of a violin playing.

"What you are listening to is the output of a microphone set up in the second tank, and to be clear, these tanks only have water in."

Some people seemed impressed, whilst others just watched on. Me, I didn't really follow, but it looked like some radio thing that could move out of one tank and into the other without any actual wires or connection, basically we're talking Bluetooth.

"We are using the excitement of signal waves in the water to transmit or move the sound output into the other tank…"

"He's reinvented the radio, nothing more," Casey grumbled to me over the Professor.

"That is impressive, Professor, but aren't you just creating your own radio waves?" Williams asked, continuing with the charade.

"Essentially, Henry, we are transmitting sound across a bonded environment by exciting the particles in the dry water. At first glance, this looks like we are merely transmitting but really, we are displacing the sound out of one tank and it is being intercepted by the other," the Professor explained.

"Right now, broadcasting sound is nothing new, but what if I told you that we have the ability to move the physical appliance across to the other tank?"

Just when the audience seemed bored, they perked up.

"If we excite both tanks enough, we can move physical items from one place to another. Do you know what that means? I'm not just saying we can move items, we can transmit near enough anything. This will revolutionise power distribution for example, wireless electricity will grant even the most remote places with light," and with that the Professor waved to his team again.

"Ladies and Gentlemen, we are at the cusp of greatness." Williams held his hands up again. The glass behind dimmed and again the tanks appeared in their neon brightness.

I could just see the dark outline of the radio. Everything flickered and for just a moment it disappeared then appeared in the other tank.

"Oh no," the Professor breathed.

"... critical failure of power..." said a voice, pretty much in a mood of 'we're all going to die'.

"Shut it down, NOW!" Ordered the Professor as he lurched towards his team.

Cameras flashed and people began to stir. The radio appeared back in the left tank and that was when the curtains began to close.

"No flash photography, the equipment is sensitive...." The Professor shouted in alarm.

"You heard the man. No flash photography," Williams bellowed, but the Press were all over this.

"Security, stop them!" he screamed.

"Guess that turned out to be a failure." Casey observed wryly, and we watched Williams' security double and then triple in numbers.

More flashes spread out from the front, whilst a pair of hired muscle men headed up onto the stage. They towered over Williams who pushed through and spoke into the microphone,

"I want them all out now, anyone who is external Press leaves now. And make sure you wipe their cameras..."

The audience gasped in outrage. This had turned ugly real fast.

"He can't do that," Casey said outraged, and sunk down into her chair.

"He is," I pointed out, just as the first big guy lurched by. He shone a torch into people's faces,

"You Press? What about you?" he barked at me.

I fumbled for my photo card and showed it just as he moved on.

"Guess I'm staying for now then," Casey added with a smirk.

At the front, a line of dark clothed security shuffled the Press away and through a fire exit. Damn but this Williams guy had made a mess. People were being roughly herded away at speed.

"Where's our own Press guy?" Williams blurted glancing up into the remaining audience.

"Have we got a Brand Outreach guy in?" he said down with what was probably his assistant.

"Wiseman," a soft voice said, but Casey had already pushed me out.

"Yeah, I'm here," I said in that throat clearing way. There I stood with a thousand judging eyes on me.

"Good. We're going to take some pictures when the Professor is ready. Nobody saw that small hiccup. This is science folks, things like this happen all the time. You ready?"

"Wiseman," Williams commanded, after his assistant repeated my name.

The Professor appeared on stage and he exchanged close words behind the security dudes covering my view.

"Okay boys, we've got it." Williams dismissed his muscle.

"We're just going to take a few photos of me and the Professor with the Displacer in the background," he instructed, and then moved out from the podium. The curtains opened and the two white coats scurried away.

Williams shuffled the Professor so that they covered the radio still sat in the left tank.

"You're using a cell phone?" he asked, and his glaring squint pretty much burned through my soul.

"Believe it or not sir, this phone has way better resolution and is connected straight to social media," I blagged. Williams' scowl turned upside down. He then nodded in approval.

My phone camera locked on and the shutter sound clicked.

"Hey! Henry! Do you want to talk about the Liqui-tech barrels found dumped off the east cliffs?" A loud and abrupt voice heckled from behind.

"Shit," I muttered. The Bitch, I mean Casey, began a power march down to me. I squinted as the bright light of her camera phone shone down.

"I'm pretty sure they were pollutants. So, your little policy is a big lie!" she continued as I covertly disappeared into a row of seats.

"What is she doing here? Get her out! Get her out of here," Williams demanded.

"So, maybe this Quantum Displacer doesn't work either… get your hands off me, that's harassment! Kurt, you're working for a lying deceiving son of a…" The two muscle men carried her out.

"How did she get in?" Williams asked and then his eyes met mine.

"Wiseman, do you know her?"

"She was sat next to me, I thought she worked here," I said, hoping it would stick.

"Yeah, she thinks she's lots of things. Journalist and sane person are two words I would not use to describe Casey Smith. She's been seeing my son with hopes of snooping around to find a story. A real try-hard type. Girls, right? Thinking they're all power these days. You got what you need in terms of pictures?" he asked.

"All good," I said, choosing not to react to what was probably a pretty sexist comment. My priority then was for a getaway with my life and career somehow intact, even if the investigative journalist/blogger/bitch across the hall almost got me in some deep doo-doo. Should I really be calling her bitch? We'll stick with Casey.

"Wiseman," Williams said again in that piercing 'you're in deep doo-doo' tone. "I think I recall that name from somewhere. Our company brochure, the cover was your handy work, right?" he asked, continuing in the same tone of 'you're sizzling on the grill right now, somebody get me outta here'.

"Yeah," I mumbled, my throat drier than a desert could be.

"Well I liked it, you got the tone of those two employees just right. People look at that image and think 'I wanna work for Liqui-tech'."

Wait, what? I mean seriously what? He liked the image, you know the guy holding a clipboard, goes home alone, masturbates etc? Then you got the broad with the fake 'get me out of here' smile and hopes just for one day nobody hits on her. Luck is a strange thing, maybe it's just my messed-up imagination. There I stood, and all I can wonder is how had that image impressed Henry Williams, the guy who basically owned my town.

"You think you could put together some more pictures for this project?"

Ah, man? Actual work? That's all I needed right now, but I had to get out,

"Sure, sounds like a good gig."

"Come and see the Professor's team and get the ball rolling. My office is open anytime," Williams oiled.

"Sure, I'll get right on that, sir," I said, continuing to cower away.

"Who are you working with up in Brand Outreach?" Williams asked

"Uh, Marcus Preston." I said.

"That idiot!" his remaining audience smirked back at him.

"Well, at least one of you guys are doing it right. Now go get that picture you snapped up on the internet and make us look good kid," he said, raising a fist as if he was trying to be inspirational.

Maybe he was in a way, he was also a sexist, commanding, overbearing dinosaur who at times and only for a second, actually made me feel good about having the job I did. It also felt dirty and wrong, kind of like a relationship you know you shouldn't be in.

Any relationship right now would have suited me.

Chapter 3: Smoke Break

I didn't want to go home, which is a revelation because normally Kurt Wiseman is the first out of the door, hotly followed by Marcus Preston. He left at lunch to help his younger wife out with the kids. He wasn't an idiot, Williams had got that wrong, Marcus did what he could to support his family, and like me, we'd both got by with no real talent. The reason I didn't want to bust out of work this time around was that I knew Casey would be waiting for me, and probably with that glare as well.

Maybe I should do some work? I know, right? Suggestions like that could end friendships. Especially the kind you and I have got going right now. It's mainly a 'you read' and I 'wear the funny clothes' deal, but aren't they all? A clever, tasteful person like you and me, both know I had to go back down there, after all that whole experiment set-up looked 'intriguing' shall we say.

In the back of my mind something told me Casey was right about Liqui-tech, and I wanted to find out more.

"Let's see if this baby is really toxic," I said to myself and moved from the open door. "Anybody home?" I called out. The communal lab coat I wore smelled of musty cologne; our Professor needed to leave that smell back in the seventies.

The dark purple slosh in those two tanks took up most of the space. They were huge, much bigger than they'd looked through the glass which had been covered by the curtain. It bothered me that somebody could just stroll in what was supposed to be a cutting-edge science set-up. Right then, nobody seemed to be home.

"I thought I would, uh… pay this place a visit and you know, take some photos," I said casually, doubting the fact any cameras would pick me up or my sound. My eyes skimmed over cables and pipes and I followed them to some desks.

"Then maybe I will sell all the plans to your competitors," I teased my audience of zero, if I knew who your competitors were. Hello dissolved radio."

My cell phone camera pointed to the shrunken radio sitting sadly inside a clear plastic crate. The same cassette radio used in the demonstration earlier.

"My guess, Detective, would be this here liquid isn't fit for human consumption," I muttered, starting to think Casey was right. This stuff had to be toxic.

"Non-pollutants my ass." I poked around at the various jars and beakers scattered about. None displayed any warning signs of being toxic; you know that little dead fish sign or an X.

"Let's take a closer look." My eyes locked onto a cluster of barrels, the only problem was that they were sitting at the top of a high ladder, on a platform, in between the tanks.

I was invested in finding something, so after taking a few more pictures from the floor, I pocketed my phone and began to climb up the cold rungs. My ears picked up a dull vibration as I moved between the glass containers, while the yellow barrels seemed to get closer the higher I climbed.

"Really need… to do… some cardio," I gasped and scrambled my way to the top. Several moments later after I'd gathered myself, I marched along the grated metal floor. From here I could see into the uncovered tanks, the liquid in those tanks from this angle looked electric blue, kinda like a sinister swimming pool.

"Bingo." I gripped the nearest yellow barrel and held it up. All kinds of danger notices were plastered around the top; I could even see that fish sign.

"Aha, that bitch was right."

My fingers slipped on some icky stickiness around the loose barrel lid. It broke free from my hand and then everything moved in slow motion.

"Nooooooo."

I stumbled with a lunge into that tunnel vision which happens when you know you've screwed up and shit is about to go down.

"Nooooooo."

My jittery eyes watched the half-empty barrel roll and spew out some brightly coloured gunk. The platform at that moment seemed to stretch a mile long and I wasn't close enough to stop this chemical crap spilling. The save came from a raised floor by the ladder.

"Phew," I breathed and hot footed my way around the spillage.

Steadily, I scooped the barrel up and put the lid back on. No one need ever know, apart from the gunk which began to drip down below that is.

"Ah man, really?" Looking around I could see nothing to mop this stuff up with. In a flash of inspiration I pulled off the musty cologne drowned lab coat I was wearing and got down on my hands and knees to throw out some serious housemaid skills, soaking up what was fast becoming a crap shower.

"Double phew," I said with relief and stood up happy with the result that my makeshift mop had now done most of the work. "It's still good."

Again, I took out my cell phone and lowered it to take an artsy type shot of the still neon water.

"That's one for the 'gram. Hashtag no filter…" And just like that, and for no apparent reason, my basic balance abilities turned full retard on me. The phone slipped out of my hand, I sprung out my other hand in preparation to catch it, but somehow I nudged it upwards instead. I staggered to a standing position hoping beyond hope that I wouldn't drop it in the drink. A wild pipe appeared to emerge from nowhere and my forehead clanged against the cold hollow metal.

"Fu…"

My vision turned tunnel and flustered again; my hands tangled in a shitty type of a juggle just as the hard edge of cell phone clipped my fingernail. The burning that ensued after crashing my head into the pipe set in and my foot stepped forward as the floor below ended. Clumsiness one; me zero and fully accepting gravity for what it was, I fell spectacularly. Arms flailing and legs open, the cell phone plopped into the murk followed by a big splash. Me.

The sound this liquid made didn't seem like an ordinary splash, an electronic echo filled my ears and I closed both eyes with a screwed-up face. My chest braced itself to feel a cold sensation, but the drink was worryingly warm. Bright flashes and then spots filled my vision, all just from closing my eyes so tight and quick, right? That's what I thought and my lips clamped together, knowing that if I drunk this stuff, the hangover would involve a casket and gravestone.

In the panic, my arms flapped and I broke the surface not daring to open my eyes. One hand brushed past something solid; my cell phone. I grabbed it groaning as my mouth opened for air. Gasping, nothing seemed to drip inside my mouth and I flopped forward with one hand. Below, my feet clunked against the glass tank and I fingered the metal grating.

Somehow, I hauled myself out with a wave of liquid splashing down below. My body lay prone to the metal grating as I gasped for air. At my feet I found my makeshift lab coat mop and finding a dry spot, I buried my head into the cloth dabbing my face constantly.

I opened both my eyes slowly to see everything in a hazy glint, unalarming in itself as this happened whenever I showered anyway.

"I'm alive, and not melting?" I murmured, realising my skin seemed fine. I pressed my fingers onto my bare chest.

"Wait, what?" My shirt was in a dissolved state and looking down I saw my jeans in tatters.

"Oh shit, I'm melting!" I shouted, the panic setting in.

"I need water!" I gagged, breathing heavily.

Down below, I clocked an emergency shower unit standing in the corner and I had to get to it.

In the rush, I didn't notice that the tank I'd slipped into wasn't the tank I'd pulled myself out of.

Chapter 4: Third Round

Waking up in my apartment. My eyes squinted at the sight of the low orange sun bleeding in through my shitty bedroom blinds.

"Huh?" The red digital numbers beside my bed formed into 5.33pm. With my bare ass facing up to the ceiling and both my legs spread out on top of the sheets, let's just take a moment to appreciate this image, as I lay there coming out of my coma. And with it, the hangover from hell.

"Uh," I groaned in a prolonged 'what the fudge happened' type of way. I'm trying to withhold the 'f-bomb' until a synonymous one-off moment later. Plus, parents of kids are less likely to spend good money on a book filled with bad language. Let's just say, any word I replace with confectionary could be a swear word.

Flapping my arms blindly around, I slapped the bedside table. Where in the Skittles did my cell phone go? I struck something light with my hand and next came a spilling sound below me. Dangling my fingers down to the rug, they brushed over loose prickles. Rice? My crusty eyes looked down confirming dry rice, and amongst the hundreds of now blue stained pellets was my cell phone.

I reached down and as my head dropped so did all the blood in my already aching melon. After a second attempt, I grabbed the cell and pulled myself back up.

"Come on, come on. Please work."

The screen glowed to life with that popular fruit shaped logo or was that the other company?

"Yeah." Victorious, I discarded the starting up device.

"Sweet Baby Ruth my head. Pee, I have to pee!" My feet scrambled the rest of my naked body up and within a second, I found myself standing at the toilet. Was I usually this quick in moving? Probably, I did have to go badly, after all.

After a marathon evacuation of dark yellow, I faced a mirror to see stubble and grease covering my face. My forehead looked bruised, or were the veins just more prominent than usual? I then poked one of the two bags under my eyes, again more veiny than usual.

"Now with extra veins," I croaked.

I noticed more and more blue blood vessels on the surface of my skin. They extended to below the neck line.

'Probably dehydration' I thought to myself, and suddenly I found myself facing the fridge, only this time I knew I hadn't walked across the whole apartment to get there.

"What?" I looked left and right. Yes, it was all still there; dirty dishes and a small table stacked with take out flyers respectively. My hand pulled the fridge door open and I grabbed a water.

I heard my cell proclaim that I'd had several messages and missed calls, so I made to head back, only before making a single step my bed jumped out of nowhere along with the room it sat in. I flinched and pulled a face not fit for public consumption.

Now I was freaked out. However, the missed call notifications took my mind away momentarily.

"Jordy, Jordy, Jordy. What the Mentos man? Just go away snake woman. Marcus work, Marcus work, shit. How long was I out?" My fingers worked quickly to the menu.

"It's Friday? Evening?"

Three damn days, that's one hell of a bender.

I briefly worked through the texts I'd missed, including a few from Marcus telling me to take the rest of the week off; sweet, because I had anyway.

Then I stared into space for a second, just to think about all the stuff you can miss in three damn days. That's a lot of clickbait personality tests in the newsfeed and I had missed them all! There were a total of twelve missed calls from snake woman Jordy and then a couple from Laura the Big L. We hadn't spoken since she'd dropped me on Monday night. Maybe I should try and smooth that over. First I needed a shower.

That's when it really hit home. My ability; you know being the Teleporter and all. Without taking a single step I'd appeared in the bathroom and was reaching for the shower dial.

"No, this cannot be happening. Really?" I closed my eyes and screwed up my face. The bright spots and sparks came again, then I thought of the kitchen.

I cautiously opened both eyelids to see the dirty dishes and takeout menus yet again.

"No way," I said shaking my head.

"Let's just have a shower and forget about it." In denial, I refused to believe I could do this and walked to the bathroom.

"See, just a hallucination or something. Booze withdrawal probably."

The blue veins didn't go away, even after a shower and second bottle of water. It wasn't a great look, maybe the oversleeping hadn't helped.

Friday night for me, normally meant a drinking session in the Drunk Poets. I really didn't feel like heading out, I had two days of fake news and clickbait to catch up on, so I kicked back and scrolled through my social media for a while.

"But I could do with a beer…" Before I had even fully stood up, the fridge faced me in what was my newly confirmed ability.

"You know 'Turk', that little trick you got ain't gonna go away," the whiny Brooklyn accent of Vinny said. In the corner of my eye the fuzzy vision of those two suits stood, you know, my debt collectors characters from New York. A cloud of cigarette smoke puffed out around them.

"It could give you real purpose in life," Lou charmed. His arm moving to adjust his trilby hat.

"Booze ain't gonna do shit for you either," Vinny added. I had already taken the chilled bottle and twisted the cap.

"What do you guys know anyway? I created you remember." I demanded, suddenly facing an empty doorway. They were gone and my eyes slid to the writing desk.

Maybe they were right, even though 'they' aren't real, my conscience is, damn my internal compass. After one sip, I placed the bottle down and even before I had moved the writing desk stood there before me.

"I'll just procrastinate some more and do something soon," I muttered. In a flash I faced my bed again. At my feet lay the discarded crumpled turquoise sweater and beside that the mostly melted denim. Luckily my prized hood hadn't been harmed and had been useful attire to wear home from Liqui-tech, still a journey I didn't remember.

I put up the hood and appeared in front of my bathroom mirror.

"I could get used to a power like this. With great power comes the possibility to go viral!" My feet spun on the spot and I looked at myself again.

"Now what will they call me?" I twirled again and assuredly stared into the mirror.

"I can travel through space instantly. I can disappear within an instant. I am... I am The Great Dissapearo!"

I squinted into the mirror, "Nope that doesn't sound right. I am, I am The Great Captain Dissapearo! But first… to the kitchen!" And as I raised a fist, the kitchen landed all around me and I sipped the beer.

"A refreshing taste and combination of hops, barley and goodness. That's why The Great Captain Dissapearo drinks premium suds," I said into where the camera could be.

"Maybe I'll head into the lounge and kick back." Again, this new ability took me onto the sofa and I lay back.

"Or I could even take a nap." This time I found myself on my bed.

"I'll probably have this super ability a while then die horribly from the poisoning, but for now The Great Captain Dissapearo must mend a bridge or two." I teleported to the sofa and grabbed my cell phone. It was time to call a friend.

"Hey Laura, Big L, how's it hanging?" I asked, always being more *street* in front of Laura.

"Kurt, where you been? I called you, hell I nearly knocked down your door. Did you skip town?" Laura asked with 'your' sounding more like 'yo'.

"Nah, man. I've been here the whole time…"

"So what? You just ignoring your friends?"

"Come on, Big L, it's not like that and look, I want to apologise about Monday. I've got something awesome to show you, come up to my apartment. Trust me, it's awesome," I encouraged, then continued to knock back beer numero uno.

"This ain't another 'awesome' wrestling cage match, is it? We watched all of those."

"Nah, Big L, this is different trust me, no cage matches. Just me and this awesome thing, I can't really describe it over the phone, just get your sweet ass up here."

"Alright son. I'm working the harbour tonight, so I'll be round before, stay tight."

"Peace out, keep it real my home girl," I beamed excitedly.

"Man, you the whitest guy I know." She laughed and clicked off.

I had to impress Laura and apologise in person. Especially as it looked like I'd chosen snake lady over her, first though, another beer. This eventually turned into three more beers before Big L came a knocking.

She stood at the door giving me *that* look, I avoided eye contact and moved back to let her in.

"What's up?" she asked, closing the door.

"Look I'm sorry about Monday, the appearance of the ex wasn't in my plans. I threw her out literally five minutes after," I said

"Alright, I'll accept, seeing as it looks like you're only a handful of beers in. The honesty stage, then comes the emotional stage. So, where you been?" The Big L interrogated me just like a suspicious parent of a kid who'd snuck home late at night.

"Nowhere, just here sleeping, 'but wait there's more'. Let me get you a beer from the kitchen, take a load off for a while." I ushered her to the sofa.

"I'll take something non-alcoholic Kurt, I'm working tonight. Stopping drunks like you from getting into trouble." She lowered herself to the sofa and I thought about heading to the kitchen.

"Let me just 'disappear' to the kitchen," I said thinking about the kitchen more, hell, I even clenched my fingers out.

Laura just stared up at me whilst I tried to do my thing.

"Did you forget where the damn kitchen is?" she asked, what with it becoming apparent my newfound ability was a 'no show'. This whole failure to perform, it's never happened in any other capacity before, not even after booze.

"Wait, just wait. It'll happen any second now," I added. The hopes were high that my Great Captain Dissapearo powers wouldn't show me up. My feet spread and I made a stance.

"I'll just go, to the kitchen," I declared dramatically.

Laura looked all around, "Who you speakin' to boy? Get to steppin', I'm thirsty."

Shit, it wasn't working. I leant down to the old cable drum that made up my coffee table and picked up the beer.

"It worked literally an hour ago. Hold on, give me a second." I stood firm and thought hard.

"Kitchen, kitchen, kitchen," I muttered.

"Look Kurt, I appreciate the apology for Monday and all, but hell knows where you've been or what you've been smoking. Probably the beer or some shit. What is that brand? I never seen that before 'premium suds'? Man, you just a drunk." Laura began to get up, so I chimed in,

"Wait, I can disappear, seriously."

She sat back again and rolled her eyes.

"Something happened on Tuesday at work. This experiment, I fell into a tank of dry water stuff. It changed me…"

"Dry water? That sounds like some bullshit. I ain't gonna believe you Kurt, especially with the track record you got. Move son, I gotta go." Laura cast me aside with one easy wave.

"Go and check in downstairs with the D-man sometime. We were worried, that woman across the hall, the B.I.T.C.H. came into the Drunk Poets lookin' for you. Maybe sober up first, sheesh." And like that, the Big L was gone.

The door slammed and I looked down at my beer. A deep thought hit me for just a second, a thought so powerful I took hold of that glass bottle and marched into the kitchen. Although this would go against everything I stood for, I turned the bottle upside down and tipped the contents down the drain.

"I can live without you. Period."

Booze, probably the main reason why I am who am, and what's that? A guy who doesn't have much. The stuff which I had come to enjoy turned out to be the main reason why my few friends didn't believe me. I'll show her and with that I flung the fridge door open. Just as I was about to grab and tip the rest away, I stopped.

"Let's not be so irrational." I slammed the door and headed out to the sofa.

"Weak man, weak…" Vinny said, vanishing as I walked through his cloud of cigarette smoke.

"I could do it earlier, trust me," I said, as if Laura was still there.

This would have been a perfect moment for my conscience, or Vinny and Lou to give me another lecture, thankfully they didn't and soon enough I found myself laying down again. My eyes closed and out I went; those three days of sleep were tiring.

This time it felt like I was out for no longer than a flash. Unexpectedly, my body lurched up into a seated position and with a dry groaning gasp I was awake.

"I need to stop sleeping so much," I grumbled and rubbed my eyes. The time now in the early hours.

In no more than a step The Great Captain Dissapearo returned and was facing the bathroom mirror. I had done it again, my powers had returned!

"The big man is back!" I shouted and felt a kind of lumpy aching at the back of my throat. Then I looked down at my clothes; turquoise sweater, jeans, all gone! My body stood naked in front of the mirror.

"Huh?" I morphed back to the sofa where my clothes lay in a pile on the floor.

"Huh? Nude Captain Dissapearo? That isn't child friendly."

I guess teleporting would take work and practice. Carrying clothes was going to be extra work.

Teleportation, Take Two, consisted of me finding a way to secure those clothes tightly to my person. I gripped both sleeves of the turquoise zip-up and tightened my belt. This time I arrived in the bathroom with the top half intact.

"Progress." Imagine the montage-type sequence of events with me working out how to keep my clothes on.

I didn't have any intention of using this stuff to become a hero, but I had come to the swift conclusion that an outfit would need to be secured to physical being, if only to avoid any naked related criminal charges.

"Jeans, tight jeans..." At the very bottom of my bedroom drawers sat the clothes I'd worn from my 'emo' rocker phase. Skin tight purple jeans, although tight they were also elastic making them comfy and unrestrictive.

Turquoise hood up, purple rocker jeans of the tight elastic persuasion: check, foot wear.

I opened my 'who gives a shit' closet, everyone's got one. That space which caters for the stuff you can't fit into. A pair of old brown boots sat at the very back behind a tennis racket, an old computer screen and various band posters which represented the very angry youth I'd once been.

"Perfect," I said, knowing they'd never fit in the first place, but they would do well for their tightness.

And Mark One of the Teleporter was born. I stood ready to head out into the night.

My objective: to prove that I could master the ability to teleport in front of Big L. My destination: the seedy quarter of Bay Valley known as the Harbour District.

Chapter 5: Breaking the Seal

A truck splashed past the front doors of my apartment block as I headed out into the drizzle. Then it turned quiet, suspiciously quiet for 2am if this were your typical crime fighting caper. Most people were asleep, but not me, I'd had plenty and so I hastily marched the short walk downhill to the sticky dancefloors and watered-down shots.

Neon lights emerged on the nearby horizon and the street turned to its pedestrian-only thoroughfare. Further ahead there were hanging baskets of lights swaying in the wind amidst a pure black backdrop of sea. For a Friday night some clubs were still going strong, for this was base hour. Anyone who had been out for the duration would now be in drunk trance mode, to me this music just sounded like a wall of noise.

Laura should be finishing up soon and probably heading my way. What club did she work in? Maybe I should text her, so I got my phone out.

I squinted at the screen and then adjusted my hood to make sure it concealed most of my face. What should I say to her? As my mind pondered this, two plastic palm trees came into view; the first bar, simply called 'Paradise' which it most definitely was not. Movement made me slow down and I watched a jumble of shadows struggle towards the street.

Two bigger guys were shuffling a much smaller looking figure. A girl. I continued to watch as these two 'big men' continued handling without care.

"Somebody probably spiked her drink."

"Well, she's the street's problem now. Maybe she'll meet a nice fella to walk her home." The pair laughed and near enough threw this girl out onto the wet street.

For a few more seconds I watched on. This girl, man she looked wasted. I heard retching before she stumbled forward into the nearby plastic palm tree of this false paradise bar.

"You need to move on lady," one of the returning 'men' said. He headed straight for her, probably with brute force in mind.

Now I said at the beginning, I am no hero. In life though, I will defend and stand up for something which isn't right. This lady, spiked drink or not, was unfit for Harbour consumption. These are seedy streets and rough times. Without even thinking I began my march, a stride of heroic proportions.

"Hey, you," my voice barked, "what are you doing to this lady?" I demanded, chest full of air and out front. "Can't you see she's wasted and probably needs a little help?"

He gripped the girl. His hand wrapped all the way around her thin arm.

"What's it to you, short stuff?" The arrogant asshole sneered and pushed the girl down. My arms tried to catch her and she sort of fell on me before reaching the wet floor.

Even with the lack of light I could see her eyes were spaced out. This had foul play written all over it.

"You're just going to throw this lady out after some heavy handling? Guys like you love to play the big Mr Important, but you ain't shit," I blurted. My words heavy with every memory of a Doorman that never let me into a place.

"Hey, Rick, everything okay?" The other muscle brain asked from the fake bamboo doorway.

"Just a small pest, I've got it," 'Rick' replied. Something then clicked. This guy and the other one at the door. I recognised them.

The drunk girl looked up at me and I helped her to stand. She retched again before blurting,

"I'm... Ta..."

"It's okay. I got you," I said, interrupting the inaudible slurring.

I then leant her against the plastic palm tree. Rick however moved closer to me with an assured smile.

"Do you want to repeat what you just said because I didn't hear it first time around, short stuff." He stood within swiping distance. It was then I noticed him pushing a button on a body mounted camera.

"Yeah," I said, and the butterflies began to swirl.

I then whispered what was probably my most badass line ever, I was on TV after all.

"You ain't worth shit..."

His frying pan sized hands were on me and they yanked at the turquoise cotton. He laid a brutal punch into my stomach and I struggled to suck air. 'Rick' then reached back and readied for another, a face shot.

"Not, today!" My words gargled as I disappeared from his grip.

Appearing behind him I faced the back of his ham-sized head as it scoped from left to right, Rick's stance let me take full advantage and I kicked like it was Super Bowl Sunday. My boot up right between his legs and he exhaled loudly in a whining pain and dropped.

"Nuts!" I shouted joyously and he near enough burst into tears. The action had begun to attract a group that were just coming out of another club. Their drunken revelry and fast food bag rustling came to an instant silence as their eyes fell on me.

"It's okay everyone, this girl needed my help," I announced and held out a hand.

"Right on," a portly looking fella nodded.

Just as Rick began his vomiting phase of the nut cracker, I stood gloating over my conquest. I had completely forgotten about the second suit, and that's when he charged me from behind.

An ice cold burning clunked over the back of my hood and I went down, express elevator style to the cold, wet floor. Those bright little sparkles began circling around my vision and then I looked up to see the other Doorman standing over me.

What did he hit me with? It still burned.

"What… did… you hit me… with…" I asked as I kinda rolled into a doggy style position.

"My fists are my only weapon," he grunted and manhandled me back up.

"Jesus, are you a damn terminator?" I asked.

"Kick the shit… outta of him," Rick demanded from his crotch clutching situation.

I knew what I had to do and even though my head felt a little woozy, I knew this guy wasn't going to win. Timing is everything in a fight, timing and running, that's how to survive and so just as another punch came my way I teleported to the sound of a curious groan from my growing audience.

Was that a light from a cell phone camera recording me?

I came back into the world less than half a second later only to find that I was at least a foot off the ground as this big bastard held me up high. As I went down my boot stumbled on a soggy sand filled bucket and its hundreds of cigarette buds that sat in a swirling black water.

Adrenalin and the urge to impress an audience drove me to pick up this damn heavy metal bucket.

My miniscule biceps stung and I raised the swirling cigarette cauldron high. Before he knew what had happened, I tipped it and its disgusting soggy contents all over his head. Let's just say the fit was snug.

Beneath the hollow metal I could hear a loud angry groan. Large hands swiped out comically whilst the audience of bar goers laughed. This comedy sequence was cut short when his flapping hands angrily caught me.

"I'm afraid that won't wash here," I said and broke the grip through teleportation.

This time the crowd even provided a golf tournament style clap.

"Did he just disappear?" one crowd member questioned.

"No, he's right there dude," another replied.

"Seriously he just reappeared behind that Doorman..."

I took a moment to look at the drunk discarded girl and remembered how they'd handled her. My fist clenched in anger and my fist reeled back. Furiously I clubbed the bucket sitting on dickhead number two's head.

"Yaowwww!" I howled, as my fist instantly turned numb, but at least the guy with the bucket helmet was out for the count.

I couldn't sell my pain to the crowd, so I put the arm behind me and faced them.

"Kurt! Is that you?" A loud and familiar voice called. Laura was standing in the centre of the group and burst through.

"Kurt? I'm afraid I do not know a Kurt for I am The Great..."

Everyone seemed to be talking amongst themselves and chatting to the Big L.

"I am The Great..." I proudly declared. Hang on, "are any of you guys listening?" I blurted.

"He literally just teleported, look I recorded it," a portly fella said. His words relaying in my head.

"Teleported? What?" Laura asked.

"Teleported," I mumbled to myself questioningly and then stood proud. "I am... the Teleporter!" I heroically declared, resting both hands on my waist.

More cell phones pointed my way and so I began to cut my promo for the world to see;

"You see, these fellas didn't treat this young lady right. I am here to make sure she gets home safe, especially as it looks like her drink was spiked. This establishment called Paradise, needs to review the way their staff treat their customers. It's okay, I'm here to help," I quickly said, cutting off the drunken girl inaudible slurred sounds.

My arms gently moved around her and in one movement, I scooped her up. This would have been a perfect moment to fly away, but was crippled by a pulsing pain that shot up my back.

"Now please, all of you, move on…" I said through gritted teeth. Laura closed in,

"You say she's been spiked?" Laura shot at me as she came closer. "Come on, my van is at the end of the block I'll get her to the hospital," and with that, I happily handed the girl over to her.

"Thank you," I grunted.

"Hey, Mr Teleport guy, do it again!" A man called from the dispersing clan of night outers.

"I only use my powers to help those in need," I called back, lapping up the attention.

"Wanna go get wasted and celebrate?" Another asked.

"Maybe some other time, shots will be on me," I smiled heroically. Then I thought of Douglas Heaney for a moment, my mentor and fellow drinksmith.

"You can find me at the Drunk Poet's society, located at the top of the hill, peace out citizens…"

"Come on, man," Laura nagged, yanking on my hood.

"Watch the attire, jeez…" I complained, following her and the girl who now seemed to be circling the sleep drain. We turned a corner and came away from the fracas.

"That place Paradise, it's run by that Williams guy. He owns a bunch of places down here. Those were his men," she said.

"I thought I recognised them. Oh well that'll teach 'em'."

"All I am saying is you can expect a receipt Kurt, and what's with this disappearing teleporter act? How'd you do that?"

"Big L, trust me when I say it's genuine, no act. Hand on heart."

"Well, whatever you did, just be careful dude. They were big mean guys back there. You coming with? Hospital is on the way past your place." Laura impressively used one hand to take out her keys and open her van side door. She then clambered in and lay the girl along a seat.

"I recognise her," I said, getting in.

"Yeah, she was with your Monday night bachelorette party." Laura got in the front and started the van.

"Tara?" I gently asked and the girl stirred.

"Huh?"

"It's okay, Tara," I said in my best heroic type accent. "You are being taken to a medical facility, it looks like your drink was spiked."

"Than...k you." Tara groaned.

Chapter 6: Tequila Baby!

I waved Big L's green van goodbye and skipped all the way into my apartment building. Nothing beat the feeling I had right then, everything felt new. Even though my head hurt and one of my hands had only just stopped bleeding, I felt great. I had even saved someone and knew then she was in safe hands with my best friend.

"I am… the Teleporter," I proudly said and looked up at the first flight of stairs.

"Let's see if these bastards can do ninety." In a flash, I reached the top. My feet skipped past a few doors and onto the next set of steps.

"Again?" And my answer came straight away as I landed on another level up.

By the time I'd reached my floor, my limitations began to emerge. The back of my throat had started to tighten and feel lumpy, a feeling of sweaty dizziness suddenly came over me.

"Powers… fading…" I said drunkenly, even though I felt sober.

My door came into view and I thudded against the opposite wall. I continued to drag myself, scraping along the wall the whole time. I stopped to gather my breath and smiled for a moment.

"Happy to be drunk again?" A voice enquired, taking me way off guard.

A face covered by blonde hair appeared from the partially open door opposite mine.

"The Bi… Casey," I said, composing myself. "And I am not drunk." I pulled down my hood.

"What happened to your hand? You're bleeding all over the hallway." Casey asked. A cardigan covered arm reached out to me and she inspected my grazed knuckles.

"Have you been fighting?" Casey's hair moved away from her face, revealing it fully.

"I could say the same about you?" I returned, referring to her bruised right eye.

She immediately covered her face up and backed up to her door.

"Who did this?" I asked, sounding like I genuinely cared. I did.

"It doesn't matter." She began to close her door when I insisted.

"Let's just say Henry Williams' employed muscle flexed on me. I got one of their names but it ain't worth pursuing. Your turn," she said pointing to my fist.

"All in the duties of being a super hero," I beamed. Casey scoffed;

"And now… what actually happened?" She folded her arms.

"Seriously, I can teleport, just not right now. I think I used up all my mojo," I delivered in a terrible rendition of an English accent. "Let me show you." I waved for her to follow me.

She adjusted her cardigan and stepped out into the hall. I ducked around her and ran through the open door closing it behind me.

"What on earth are you doing Kurt?" she demanded, unamused.

"Hi there, something wrong with the door?" I teleported beside her and Casey jumped.

"Shit!" She half screamed.

"Neat, right?" I laughed, disappearing again.

"Where did you go?"

My trembling hand opened her apartment door and I shuffled out.

"Just inside your place. Not a bad layout," I teased. Casey frowned for just a moment and then barged past me.

"Look. I don't know what cheap trick you're playing but I don't want to know. I've already got one black eye." And like that, she slammed the door.

"Suit yourself. Justice isn't for everyone. Geez." I muttered, and walked into my apartment.

She's just freaked out a little. Hell, I was at first. She'll be back. So I put my feet up and decided to watch some much needed therapy of two grown men throwing each other off a twenty foot plus cage.

Just when I began to doze off, a firm knocking sound came from the door.

"I knew it," I said smirking to myself, and before I could greet my more than expected guest, she butted right in.

"I get the exact same bottle of tequila every year from my grandparents who live down in New Mexico. I've never touched the stuff but right now I think I need some and you also need to tell me your story." Casey stood holding in her hand the holy grail of spirits. She then showed me the screen of her cell phone. A blurred image of a guy wearing the exact same hood as me punching a bucket wearing doorman.

"I'll grab some glasses. Some salt and some lime."

I teleported to the kitchen and by the time I came back, Casey was sitting down with her arms folded. Her unimpressed face was frowning at the sight of two men grappling atop of a wire cage.

"Everyone who's about to say, what you're about to say; I show them this match," I said over the loudness of an arena audience from 1998.

"So, are they going to fight in the cage?" Casey asked.

"Just watch," and I sat down and joined her. In my hands I held a tray with all the condiments required. Everyone should have a home tequila kit. She grabbed a shot glass and began to pour.

"But the ring is inside the cage?" she asked, trying to understand.

As usual whenever I show this wrestling match to somebody outside the fanbase 'circle' of sports entertainment, I watch them react in disbelief.

"Oh my god." Casey's eyes couldn't look away.

"Uh… you're spilling it." I grabbed the overfilled shot glass.

"These guys disprove the whole 'fake' deal," I grinned and then we clanged shot glasses.

"Salt…" Casey chugged the sourness back.

"Lime… blurgh." She shuddered.

"This is good stuff but tequila has a way of biting you back, for people of a certain age that can be a game changer," I pointed out and licked the salt, you know the rest.

"People of a certain age? What does that mean?" Casey asked.

"Mid-twenties."

"So late twenties then. Me, well it isn't polite to ask a lady such things. Another?" She was already pouring another shot.

"Lady?" I dared.

Her loosened up stare flashed into a glare for just a second.

"I guess one more will be okay." I accepted the shot.

"Are you going to show me that disappearing act again?"

"Doesn't work after booze which is a major bummer," I admitted.

"Booze is your kryptonite. Hah, way to stay healthy. I don't usually drink; I'm a yoga person," Casey said. Again, we drank. "He's climbing up on the cage again. Is that guy like dead these days?"

"Mrs Foley's baby boy? Nowhere near. Are you ready to tell me what happened with your eye?" I asked

"I told you, Kurt. Henry Williams' hired muscle roughed me up on the way out of Liqui-tech. They know I'm a reporter. Well, that's history for now, there's no amount of cover up that will cover this and I'm pretty sure he's told every editor in town to blackball my stuff. So that's depressing," Casey said. For a moment there, I thought the water works were coming and she bowed her head.

"I just wish there was some way to expose that bastard for who he really is," she added and for the first time, I saw a fire in her eyes.

"Well maybe I can help for I am, the Telepor...."
As I sprang up so did a searing electrical type shock that ran along my spine.

"Damn my back..." I moaned and crashed back to the sofa.

If I stayed still it didn't hurt.

"Sounds like you need some yoga in your life."

"There's that word again. *Yohhga*, is that like a yoghurt juice drink or something?" I asked. The searing pain slowly bleeding away. "Seriously though, Casey, I can help. I work for the company

Williams owns. He has to have something incriminating in his offices," I added.

"He owns multiple firms in the valley Kurt. I don't know exactly what we are looking for."

"Well Casey, the fact is, you were right. The stuff Liqui-tech uses is toxic." I reached for my cell phone and swiped until a photo came up, the barrel full of gunk.

"You see? That's a start," I said.

She seemed more interested in the chemical staining surrounding the screen case.

"What have you and your cell phone been rolling in?"

"Stuff... for science. But look, that barrel full of gunk, it's gotta be toxic right?" I asked.

"We need more to make a case for this guy." Casey said, still unconvinced.

"I say we bust in there at sunrise-ish, Saturday morning. The place will be deserted, take some more photos and check out his offices. If there's one thing I know about these sorts of things, it's the simple fact that there's probably a filing cabinet unlocked and it's full of incriminating stuff just waiting for us to find!"

"Well, talking of incriminating, what about this video of a guy shaped just like you making the rounds on social media?" Casey showed me the pixelated video yet again.

"That could be anyone wearing a turquoise hood. Viral stuff goes stale after a day, tomorrow I'll be plain old Kurt yet again."

I couldn't have been more wrong.

Another round and then the yoga unfurled.

"Urgh. It... feels... good..." I gasped. My left arm reaching upwards and then the pain adjusted.

"This is called Warrior One," Casey said. I heard a whistle from her nose as she took in a deep breath.

"Now inhale... and twist your arms to your side," she instructed, making this crap look easy.

The sore burning of my lower back pain seemed to dissolve from the various suggestive poses I'd followed from Casey. So, it was good crap, for now.

"Deep breaths."

"I'm trying..." Something clicked and with it came ultimate relief.

"I think, you have exercised the demon," I groaned, crashing back onto the sofa, which became my bed until late-morning when Casey launched a rolled-up yoga mat my way.

"Now can we go and corporate espionage?" I pleaded.

"This is the perfect way to start a day. Warrior One and, slowly adjust into Warrior Two," she said.

"I'm more of a keyboard warrior type." I miraculously got up without pain.

"Do we have a plan? An actual motive of why we are going to snoop around Williams' offices?" Casey moved her yoga mat onto my cluttered floor. She seemed to have put all my mess in neat organised piles.

"I got a few ideas. My boss Marcus, he has a history with Williams, a long and complicated backstory intertwined with affairs, alcohol and fast women," I said.

"Seriously?"

"Nah, I don't know, but there's something lurking just under the surface of Williams' empire and we are going to find it."

"And how are we getting into his offices?"

"Well, Casey, I just happen to be the Teleporter. And I work there, and you just happen to be an angry, ticked off investigative journalist looking to expose a business asshole."

"A capitalist asshole president supporting chauvinist who thinks he has the key to this town. Newsflash is… I'm about to change the locks," Casey said with the last word.

And like that we found ourselves nearing the top floor of Liqui-tech in a plush staircase.

"Executive stairs now available in carpet," I triumphantly observed.

"You can probably take some of that get-up off now, Kurt."

The Teleporter Mark Two had seen a few additions to the original outfit. This included a purple bandanna which covered my face below a pair of cool sunglasses. The hood remained and this time a biker style jacket covered most of the turquoise.

"We probably shouldn't use real names," I said climbing the last few stairs. My body clumsily crashed straight into the closed door leading to Execland.

"Maybe the shades and hood combo would work if you could actually see." Casey moved in front and opened the door. We stepped onto more carpet.

The lights clicked on with our movement suggesting nobody was lurking around the place. They lit up the office which stretched the length of the building. Further up I saw a glass wall.

"Well where do we start?" Casey asked. I had already found a distraction.

"They have a coffee machine, a free coffee machine? So they've got carpets and free beverages whilst we slum it downstairs on a regular plastic floor. That's the real injustice here..."

"Kurt!"

"It's this way," I grumbled. We moved past cosy office cubicles and headed toward the glass wall which revealed itself to contain an office.

'Liqui-tech' was etched across the dark glass. Henry Williams' office; it had to be. My hand gripped the metal door handle and it opened inwards.

"That was too easy," I whispered, just as some expensive lamps came to life.

"Well that makes sense, to be surrounded by his own kind," Casey said, pointing to a wall-sized display of dinosaur bones.

"Is that a mini bar…?"

"Kurt! The mission, right?"

"Right." I zig-zagged to a glass desk bigger than my bedroom. Then I stopped dead,

"You hear that?"

"Hear what?" Casey asked, standing at a varnished shelf unit stacked with books.

"A ringing in my left ear." I popped a finger in and out of my ear; the ringing temporarily stopped whenever I blocked it.

"Can't hear a thing. I'm not seeing any filing cabinets full of evidence Kurt."

"If this guy had any sense he wouldn't have anything incriminating sitting around," I said. My attention turning to the huge reclining leather chair.

"Jesus, this is soft and firm in all the right places." I kicked up my boots onto the solid glass table. They crumpled a bunch of papers as I got comfortable. "I could get used to this." The ringing in my ear bothered me, so I didn't stay still for long and breezed out of the door.

"It's pretty damn empty in here."

"I guess we need to dig deeper." I stood over the nearest desk, his secretary's I presumed. This seat near enough spooned my lower half with soft to the touch leather.

"Nope this isn't right." My knees were too high, the owner of this seat had it all wrong or maybe they were just short, so I bent forward and reached for a handle. My hand waved around until I felt something just out of grasp. "Why do they make these things like this?"

I wheeled forwards and grabbed the handle. I began to elevate with an airy squeak from below, my head in brace position and then, crunch.

"Aww shit," I swore. The underside of the desk collided with my head and I became wedged forward underneath it.

"A little help maybe?" My voice box squeaked in the crush.

"Quit fooling around Kurt."

"Seriously. I'm stuck damn it..." Casey pulled the chair free and I flopped to the floor. My eyes looked up at her from my hidey hole.

"There's something over here." She had already gone before I'd struggled to get up.

"Wait up," I said, seeing Casey standing in front of a plain wooden door.

She tried the door handle and it clunked as a lock held.

"What do you think? Supply cupboard or something else?" Casey asked, nudging the door with her shoulder.

"Let's find out." I sized up the door.

"Can you just teleport in there?"

"Nope, haven't been in there before so I can't."

"What type of teleporter are you?"

"A useless drunk teleporter with back problems," I admitted.

"Look I'm still figuring out this stuff, the basic rule is this. Any distance is hard and anywhere I haven't been is out, no chance…"

Casey forced the door open with a firm shoulder barge. And what stood in the shimmering light in front of us you ask? Not one filing cabinet, but a whole damn records room stacked with them.

"Let me be the first to say, Bingo," Casey declared and headed for the nearest grey metal cabinet. With zero persuasion, the top drawer slid open.

"Let's get to work," I said, locking on to another cabinet.

"I still don't know what we are looking for, but I'll know it when I see it," Casey said and began rifling through files.

Yeah and I know, this whole deal is paper thin. We just happen to bust in and find some stuff to pin on our apparent bad guy. The motive gods were stirring. I'll agree with you there and go out on a limb to say this may have been too good to be true.

"This is all just boring old paper work," I said. Surprisingly the next cabinet I opened contained more folders and papers.

"Bureaucracy is how conflicts are resolved these days. Businesses hide behind themselves forgetting about what they leave behind, every firm in this great nation has to keep a record of its past. Even in the digital age."

"You may wanna tidy up that little paper trail you left," she suggested. I faced the half-open cabinets and saw paper everywhere.

"Nah, I'm good. As far as we're concerned we weren't here," I said and shoved a drawer shut.

Casey pulled another cabinet wide open and that's when we saw it.

"You see, what I see?" Casey asked as she opened another file.

"It's beautiful." I stood mesmerized by the potential incriminating goodness. I got a closer look and Casey pulled off my shades, and continued to scan the document.

"But this can't be," I said with disbelief.

"What is this?" I asked. My eyes skimmed over various key words in what looked like legal and financial jargon.

"This here is leverage. Oh, this asshole is gonna get blown wide open," Casey said. She pulled out her cell phone and the photo shoot began.

"And it's going directly to the cloud."

"Uh, I'm not sure the cloud is the best place for this sort of thing Casey," I disagreed.

"It's not like they are nudes or anything, lighten up," she replied.

Cue the short montage of Casey taking photos whilst I suggestively posed just out of frame.

"We should probably bounce," I suggested. My lips touched the paper cup and I sipped free machine coffee, the best kind.

"Yep, okay. I just wanna poke around downstairs before we go. Take a look at that experiment for myself." Casey gently pulled the records room door shut.

"I say we just bounce. We got enough." I followed little Miss Determined back past the cubicles.

"Nope. I'm headin..." Before she pushed on the staircase door it opened.

"Shit," I muttered, and some voices followed by people intercepted us.

Casey tried to bow her head away and ignore the obvious asshole looking guy leading some other stoner type through to us.

"The conference room is pimped out y'all, surround sound..." the first guy said and then trailed off as he met us.

"Yo, what are you doing here?" he asked.

"Look man it's the dude from that sick video." The stoner fella pointed straight at me as he held a six pack of beers.

"Toby, if you'll excuse me," Casey said.

She knew him? The first guy? She tried to move past him, however 'Toby' gripped the doorway.

"I asked you a question, Casey. What happened to your face?" he demanded.

His hand reached out and tried to brush her fringe away.

"Your Father's security cronies. That's what happened, now move," Casey ordered. She kept her eyes down and attempted to barge past.

"Who's your friend?" The arrogant half-smile of Toby faced me.

"It's the Teleprompter y'all," the stoner dude said. "That video was badass man."

"It's the Teleporter," I said, correcting him.

"You're the guy who took out my old man's security guys. Nah, wait man." Toby stepped in and pushed me back.

"And you're the guy with the loud car that Casey broke up with, right?" I shoved back. This guy's loud revving from five floors below had put my alarm clock out of a damn job.

"And what? The car's a classic. Maybe I should give the old man a call, let him know you're trespassing on private property," Toby argued. He snatched out at me and pulled on the jacket I wore over the turquoise hood. "Or maybe I could deal with you myself."

This asshat can't touch me, yeah, I said asshat. It's an ass in a hat and I'm a viral video hero. In a flash, I teleported behind him and raised my bandaged fist.

"NO! Stop!" Casey stepped between us and pushed my clenched hand back.

"So you do still care about me, huh?" Toby asked Casey. His slimy face smiling in that assured 'my daddies got a lot of money' way.

"Stop," Casey said. She avoided his eyes in every way possible. I sensed some shame, maybe I'll gently ask her about it sometime.

"You better keep the 'Teleporter' on a short leash Casey, or you'll both get hurt. Come on Dash," Toby said and did his best to barge past us.

"Whatever silver spoon," I said.

Casey rushed for the stairs and I followed.

"Yeah, we should like, go." I jumped the steps down, catching up with Casey.

"After we checkout downstairs," she said up to me.

"But you heard what he said right? He'll tattle on us to his Daddy," I called down.

"If there's one thing I know, Toby Williams is a professional bullshitter. And you're the Teleporter. I'm relying on you to literally get us out of any shit."

"Right on, I guess. What was all that about anyway?" I asked.

"Toby and I went out, he pretended to be someone else. I found that out; the end."

"Gee… don't skimp on the detail or anything."

We rushed the rest of the way down to the lobby level in silence. On a Saturday it was normally a ghost town. And like our arrival earlier, nobody was around.

The conference theatre doors were closed when we got there, so I covertly opened them.

"Let me just check to see if the coast is clear," I whispered.

My eyes peeked through a gap in the double doors.

"What do you see?" Casey asked.

"There's something happening in there. Come on, stay down," I told her, knowing she wouldn't just turn away at the sight of people.

I crawled into the theatre with Casey close behind me until we reached the seats.

"Looks like they are cleaning." My eyes squinted to the various white coats crawling all over the two-tanks full of liquid.

"They are scrubbing it," Casey whispered.

"Perhaps we should go." She turned.

"No, stay!" A slithering voice said from above us.

I stared up wide-eyed to see the gloating Henry Williams in a tracksuit. Either side of him stood an entourage of muscle framed in the open doors. We were in shit street right next to crap alley in the town of excrement.

"Trespassing is a criminal offence Miss Smith. You already know that," Williams glowered. I had already begun to move up onto my feet.

Casey jumped up and flung an arm around mine. I clenched my hands in preparation to teleport.

"Get us out…"

Before she could even finish the sentence, we were in the lobby, all clothes intact.

"… of here."

That same lumpy feeling in my throat led in to a tired dizziness which overcame me.

"Come on," Casey urgently tugged on me and I came out of the daze. That was the furthest I had ever Teleported and with a passenger. Now I was pooped.

"Get them!" Williams called, and feet squeaked on the marble flooring, they were coming for us.

"We need to go Kurt, teleport us anywhere. Come on!" Casey cried and gripped my hand again.

"I'm, trying…"

I groaned and clenched. For a flash, we vanished. The first meathead stumbled to the floor but it wasn't enough, my power had faded and we didn't go anywhere.

"Run instead?" Casey pulled at me and everything moved slowly. A huge wave of sleepiness gripped me long before any bumbling tanned and tattooed private security could.

"Get off!" she screamed.

Two eyes looked down into my shades.

"You in there?" The beefy security guy enquired.

Before I could even throw a single punch, something hard hit me.

I blacked out.

Chapter 7: A regretful bar selfie

The reverberating bass of male voices stirred me. I heard that same ringing in my ear again and this time it really got to me. More talking fired back and forth in argument until I fully came to. Another hangover kicked my ass and a headache from hell put me all over the place.

"What's going on?" I asked. My body rigid, I couldn't move.

"Let's see who this hoodlum really is," the voice of Henry Williams shouted angrily.

Someone yanked my head back and I felt the soft breeze of air conditioning. I was exposed as the turquoise hood lowered back onto my jacket.

"Take the other stuff off too!"

The shades were ripped from me and the bandanna covering most of my face got roughly lowered. Now I was awake and two squinting eyes were burning into me.

"You? The Brand Outreach fella? Well, you're fired," Williams said. He eased into the big boss seat behind his big boss desk.

"Wiseman, wasn't it?"

"It's the Teleporter," I said through gritted teeth.

"Hah, that damn name. I have had enough of that damn name. All day I've been hearing it. From what I can gather, that little ability you find yourself using is property of Liqui-tech. So, I own your clown ass. As a matter of fact..."

"You don't own shit!" In the corner of my eye I could see a red-faced Casey, she was strapped to a chair like me.

"Maybe I should add false imprisonment to the list of crimes this bent company is associated with," she added.

Williams didn't budge from his power posture and squinted her way,

"Miss Smith, you and your friend here were trespassing. I was merely apprehending you for the authorities. That's the story we're gonna go with anyway. You see I've dealt with your kind many times before. Most men have, but eventually you'll find your place. This isn't the first time a silly little girl like you has snooped around the place and spread lies." He raised a finger before Casey could interrupt, probably to call him a sexist pig. He was.

"This room though, it's solid. Nothing can penetrate these walls, even the glass; that's special tempered stuff." He held both his palms out before clambering up from the chair like an upturned bug.

"You can feel it can't you, *Mister* Teleporter?" he sneered at me.

My eyes locked onto his and he crept my way.

"Why don't you go ahead and try to teleport out of this one. Go on, try. I'm curious to see it in action. After all this is my creation; YOU are my creation."

"Get us out of here Kurt," Casey pleaded.

I clenched both fists and tried to wrestle my arms free. They were lashed to the armrests with silver duct tape. The back of my throat ached and I began to strain.

"You hear that ringing? What about now?" Williams asked.

An unholy white noise filled both my ears.

"Ahh! God make it stop!" I screamed.

In Williams' stubby hand I saw a remote control.

"If you say so," he said and the ringing abruptly stopped.

"You see this room is built like those tanks downstairs, you know, the Quantum Displacer port you contaminated? Professor Rice used that tech to make my office bonded, for security reasons. No signals transmit in or out so that little power of yours is obsolete in here. It also stops little 'try hard wannabe' reporters prying where they shouldn't. Pretty neat, huh? They wired it in with the air con, Well what's this?" he asked. I felt his slithery hand pick at the pride badge I wore on my chest.

"A pride badge," I said, like he should know.

"Well that does explain a lot," he snorted jeeringly at me.

"Actually, it doesn't. You see the world is only gonna change when people like me also start wearing badges like this one," I argued to the prehistoric opinionated prick.

95

"That crowd are just trouble. How can you employ someone who's going to cause that much…"

"If you don't mind, Mr Williams. Could you turn that remote back up? I'm done hearing your shitty girly voice," I said, knowing I would regret it but I could never pass up a chance to be cute so the ringing came back worse than ever.

"Ahh… that's the spot!" I groaned with feigned pleasure. My body began to shake and spasm.

"You're itching a big time scratch, just there…"

"Stop it!" Casey ordered. Just before I blacked out Williams casually adjusted the frequency back to normal.

"It's funny how a stupid little drunk girl can cause a world of problems for a businessman like me. You did a number on my guys outside Paradise, I'll admit that. That's one of my businesses. You also made it look bad, you told lies about the place and the problem is these days I can't intercept fake news like that. If I didn't own so many of the local news outlets they would be having a field day right now, all because of a stupid little drunk whore," Williams barked, his words turning spiteful.

"She's not a whore. Her name is Tara and somebody in that place you own spiked her drink. Nobody in there took care of her…"

"Get him out of here, I've had enough of his stupid greasy face. I'll deal with him another time."

Williams waved me away as large hands gripped me. The tape holding me down got slashed and I was up.

"As for you Miss Smith, why don't you stay a while."

"You can't just hold me here against my will. That's against the law," Casey shouted.

"That's funny, the last time I checked, I own most of the law in this town. Ah, your sunglasses Mr Teleporter," Williams called to me. The muscle heads dragging my ass turned me back.

Just as I got in reaching distance of the shades he dropped them to the floor.

"Whoops. Better pick them up," he said with a fake capped teeth smile.

The grip behind me loosened and I eased down to the carpet. My hand closed in on the shades when Williams stomped on them. He twisted his foot and before I could look up, he drove a kick straight into me.

"You bastard!" Casey shrieked. I fell back in a daze.

"This whole Teleporter fad, it's over before it began. Drunk people don't need a voice, people in general don't need your voice. Consider yourself shut down."

I clutched my chest in protection from another cheap shot, but his damage was done. All that viral video hero stuff drained away.

"Get him up!" They pulled me to my wobbling feet.

"In this town you're nobody, you're just some viral prank I set up. That'll be the real story they'll all hear anyway. Remind Mr Teleporter here of what happens if you mess with my security," Williams ordered. He spun away and then swung straight back at me with a sucker punch, right in the gut.

Something told me deep inside not to sell the pain, I gasped anyway.

"As for you Miss Smith, we're going to have a little one-to-one talk. I'm in two minds about summoning the authorities, maybe I should just deal with you personally."

"No, damn it. You son of a bitch," Casey cried and I couldn't help her.

Another blunt force crashed into my stomach and then came a scratching burn which flashed across my lip. I fell to the carpet in a drunk-type of confusion. They dragged me away.

Chapter 8: I vape now

Everything hurt. Even stuff I didn't know I even had. And yes, so did my nuts, although they hadn't taken a direct hit because my tail had stopped that as it sat firmly between my legs. So, as they hurled me out of a van and onto the wet sidewalk, I looked up to the near dark sky. They had probably beaten me to only a few inches from death. That's how all of these emotions felt anyway.

I dabbed the fresh cut on my lip with a finger and then moved to the bruising around both eyes. All I wanted to do right then was crawl away down a hole and disappear forever. Just as the Teleporter had arrived he'd got chopped down and beaten. Maybe if this were a feature film 'behind blue eyes' would be playing, or that 'half the man I used to be' song. Either way, I just stayed there on the wet sidewalk, defeated. It was all over so quick. For me only hours had passed since I had become the Teleporter and now, that image of helping people sat in ruins.

"He's been laid out on his ass big style," Vinny said. I didn't have time for his whiny voice tonight.

"Looks like a professional job as well," Lou added, unsympathetically.

"Maybe we should take him downtown. Sit him in the drunk tank for the night, keep him outta trouble." Vinny took a long drag before flicking the cherry red cigarette end away.

"You're forgetting one thing, Vinny. We ain't been PD for three years now, I say we leave him be. Let sleeping dogs lie and all."

And like that the pair headed towards a brown Buick. A bus hurtling water my way broke my trance.

Through the pain of those various wounds, some physical but a lot that was mental, I hauled myself up and limped to the nearby steps. They led down to that familiar deserted bar where all my woes could be forgotten. Was I ready to face Douglas? Not yet, so I sat on the top step for a while, the cold breeze hitting my wet clothes.

"I'm fired, well shit," I said.

Coming to terms with losing a decent paying effortless job hurt, although the wounds of being shut down and told I'm no longer the Teleporter ran deeper. All because that one night of saving Tara and taking out two meatheads may have been the most selfless thing a drunk could do, and I'd been sober at the time.

Those people heading home to nurse a hangover the next day, I was their symbol. A symbol that nights out won't be ruined by people spiking drinks in seedy clubs and that 'security' won't just walk all over you. Those values, they stood a distance from now. Those values were before they got me beaten up and fired. Were they even worth fighting for?

Maybe people like me are just born to lose. People like Henry Williams have the money and have the power to say and do what they like. In an instant, they can crush low levellers like me. We'll just medicate on whatever fills that emptiness of knowing we can never win. The media will distract us under our noses and in plain sight to convince us this life is just them winning every damn time.

I looked down into the Drunk Poets. Only now I could see people, lots of people.

Before I even got down to the door it opened to the cheery greeting from Laura,

"He's here, ya'll! Told ya!" She announced back to an entourage of people spread about the place. They cheered at my arrival and over the threshold I went. Then I put up my hood to cover most of my facial damage.

"Ah, Kurtis! I could kiss you, you beautiful feckin' bastard!" Douglas came my way and wrapped his arms around me. The fresh bruising was tender. I gasped in pain as he handed me a bottle.

"Have a drink, you deserve it. I can call you by your name, right?" he asked.

"They are all here to see you man. The Teleporter," Laura grinned.

I couldn't embrace the atmosphere. This was all false, I was false with a false following. I'm nobody, even to the people scattered around drinking, talking and laughing. Having a good time in a good bar.

"Hey Mr Teleporter guy? Can I get a photo?" A guy asked and with him a group of golf outfit wearing party goers.

I turned and saw the flash before I even looked into the cell phone camera.

"Shots! Shots! Shots!" Another group chanted loudly from the bar.

"We got one for the Teleporter right here!"

Just then, this whole deal seemed strange and out of place, or just plain inappropriate. I had just been humbled to the ground by a corporate dinosaur and beaten to within an inch of my life.

All these people had come to see me, but what was I symbol of? Drinking? The one thing that I couldn't do if I wanted to be the Teleporter. This was my medication to distract me and others that people like Henry Fucking Williams control the world. Free speech or not.

"You showed those stupid bouncers a thing or two, man. Am I right? High five dude."

And yes, I held my hand up for the guy. Under the hood I wasn't so celebratory. I mean yeah, I was happy for Douglas to have the customer influx.

I took a single swig of beer, the sourness mixing with the blood in my mouth.

"Hey, Turk man. I've got that girl Tara on facetime right now. You wanna say hi?" Laura asked and pushed her cell phone in my face.

The smiling resemblance of Tara faced me in its pixelated glory.

"Hey, Mr Teleporter. Thanks for saving me last night, maybe we should go out sometime?" she asked so innocently, nobody knew the truth.

I was just a guy who accidently fell in a tank of chemicals and then got fired. The guy who would never win, especially to those with money, power and greed. Maybe I've laid it on thick enough that you realise this is politically loaded. At that moment, I was still finding a reason to be this symbol.

Right then the room just seemed to spin, people's eyes were on me. Camera flashes, taps on the shoulder, I had to bust out of there, it was too much.

From behind me came a ringing in my ear and I lowered myself for a moment, only to realise Douglas was standing on stage at the microphone.

"Now, I know why you are all here and it's to see that man there. Give it up for the hero of drinkers everywhere, the Teleporter!"

People clapped and patted me on the bruised shoulder, and all for what? Making sure a drunk girl got home okay? What made me deserve this? Before I knew it, I was talking on stage.

"Look," I said and stood for some moments. I then lowered my hood to reveal a probably beaten face.

"He's been fighting!"

"For us!"

"Look," I said again.

"This whole Teleporter deal, has got way out of hand too damn quickly. That stuff you are drinking, it's just poison and it's no good for anything. Everyone has their escape, a distraction from what's happening in the world. Booze isn't the damn answer." My audience gasped in synchronisation as I spoke.

"Nah man, booze is the damn cure!" A loud guy said from the back to a wave of cheers.

"I'm not some super hero. I'm just a guy who tried to do the right thing. The Teleporter is just a fantasy of mine. It's not real, none of this is. Go home, be with your friends and family. Appreciate what you got. Either way you'll lose it all, eventually." And that was the mic drop of all mic drops.

"Wait! What's goin' on?" Laura asked. In a daze, I filed past the people.

"Big L, this isn't how I imagined it would be. I have to be alone for a while," my croaking voice said. I looked into her frowning eyes; she could see this was genuine.

"Text me son," she said.

In the corner of my eye I could see Douglas pouring something into a line of punter's mouths.

"Good for him," I said softly and made my exit.

Yep, things got deep and reflective. Even though that could be the title of a porno, it wasn't, I don't think. Let me tell you something, this story ain't no picnic and right then I hated myself. Even though this is supposed to be about heroes and triumph, first there's the knockdown, then comes the supposed climb and the fight back. Just then it was come down central.

With the sour taste of beer and blood in my mouth, I began to hate the idea of booze and what it did to me. My beaten body dragged itself up several steps until I trailed back to the retreat of my apartment. The couch consumed me as I sat in a slouch of defeat and I tuned out momentarily.

But I still needed something to 'fuzzify' things. Even with all the booze resentment, an addict is always an addict. The craving conflicting with desperation always finds a way. That half bottle of tequila left over from last night. Yeah, I know, weak but it would do the job.

My hand pulled it free from between couch cushions and I brushed the television remote control. Voices and brightness blared at me.

"Not true, not true. Those are just false facts. The real facts are this." I instantly recognised the echoing voice of Henry Fudging Williams coming out of the TV.

"This was all an elaborate publicity stunt to spread awareness of what can happen in certain establishments in the Harbour District. The Teleporter is a creation by my wonderful Brand Outreach guys at Liqui-tech. The young lady, Tara, perfectly fine and a wonderful actress. The violence, staged, all staged..."

"Ah bullshit!" I launched the bottle into the TV. Channel something news went off in a flash along with the crappy skype call the anchor woman was having with that asshat.

My mind receded into silence and rested toward nothingness. I began to nod off when there came a knocking at my door.

"Go away," I yelled.

The knocking didn't go away and with it came a muffled voice,

"Kurt, it's me Casey."

"Kurt isn't here right now," I said.

In my mind, I was a little relieved she'd got back safely, only now came the resentment of the trouble she'd got me in.

"Well, if you could give the message to Kurt. Tell him I'm sorry, I feel kinda responsible for getting him fired. If he wants to help still, I'm going to pursue the evidence we got today at Liqui-tech," she said, I could sense her turning away from the door.

"Whatever," I called back and rolled over on the couch. In my ear came the slamming of her apartment door.

Fade to black because that was where I stayed for the rest of the night and day. I didn't exactly have work to get up for anymore.

Chapter 9: A regretful text message

A depressive slump of nothingness hung over me until eventually I decided moving forwards and away from thoughts of failure was my only solution. Doing a bunch of stuff got me through the next few days and away from my failed super hero mode.

Doing 'stuff job number one' consisted of peeling off my partially blood-stained outfit and launching it at my laundry chair. Everybody has a laundry 'chair' and for some people it even takes the form of a once used exercise bike.

Smaller tasks drove me on, like straightening the place up and doing the laundry, they provided a much-wanted distraction away from thinking. Screw what happened back at Liqui-tech, lets live in the now.

My cluttered apartment began to clear, except every time I took something else up off the floor Casey's damn yoga mat taunted me. I would bend over and grab something, only to find it sniggering at my burning back pain.

I began searching yoga stuff online until I finally mustered up the courage to roll out the mat. Weird stretching poses distracted me further and opened up my mind to other thoughts, like the short term and my creative aspirations. Yeah, even a bum like me has those.

More important stuff like getting a job or leaving the apartment intrusively came to mind, at least the fridge was stocked enough to buy me a few days. My savings were good for a few months along with the rent, and so I found for the first time in what seemed like forever, time to draw and write, and relax with yoga.

I happily sat in my apartment letting the world go by whilst I sketched the next characters of my masterpiece. When I hit a wall, I simply stretched it out on the mat. Hell, I even smiled a few times, especially when the back pain went. Slowly my body became stronger. Days passed and every so often the thoughts of failure flashed back at me, only now each time now more diluted than the last.

"You gotta appreciate there ain't many people who actually see themselves in the mirror for real," the arriving Vinny pointed out. I hadn't seen either of those guys from 'One Night' in a while.

My fist thumped loudly on the desk and the image of Vinny fizzled away. Expressing physical anger worked sometimes.

"Just don't think about it," I commanded myself.

Just when I'd got myself back into the swing of sketching another voice bothered me,

"You know you can't hide in here forever. You gotta face stuff head on," Lou's deep voice rumbled.

My knee began to bounce as more and more thoughts repeatedly pestered me by way of Lou and Vinny chattering in either ear.

"Damn it," I said, rolling my chair back. Why was this shit bothering me now? "Come on dude, keep it together," I told myself, pacing.

"Yeah. You fall apart, so do we…"

"Shut up!" I shouted and swung for the disappearing figure. Over my shoulder he appeared again.

"You gotta face facts, kid. This whole hero charade is part of something bigger."

I sat down and slumped onto the couch. The bruising had all but healed from being assaulted by Williams and his cronies.

"I'm just taking a load off, not moping or slumping. Just resting before another sketch or two," I said.

"But what about motive?" A buzzing voice whispered into my ear. I jumped up and swatted away the invisible pest.

"Motive?" I asked.

"Remember that word? That's what every story relies on," another voice wheedled.

"Screw this," I said and grabbed a jacket. Out the door I went, my feet walking me away from these unwelcome thoughts.

I needed to think; I knew I wanted revenge. First off, I had to go and find Williams. But real life isn't that easy and decisions made that affected others' lives needed clear thought. Plus, there was more.

That word 'motive', it kept burning in my mind, even as I strolled into the Harbour District, the place seemed somehow less busy that night. Even the Paradise Club looked shut when I moved along the wet sidewalk. I found myself leaning over the barrier, staring at the crashing waves as I looked down at the black sea water. A strong sea breeze blew into my face forcing me to turn out of its path. A wet rippling flapped against my ear.

"Huh?" I pulled away a sheet of soggy newspaper that had jumped up at me.

"Does the world need a figure like the Teleporter?'" I read the title of the article out loud. My eyes focused on a blurred resemblance that could have been me, printed next to a bunch of writing.

"That's the million-dollar question," I muttered.

"You know, son," the voice of an old man said, "people will always look for the hero in life. It gives people hope and makes the world seem like anyone can still achieve their dreams." If he'd got any closer, I think I could have got drunk just from the fumes on his breath alone.

He placed two wrinkly hands on the barrier and looked down to the water. I recognised him from somewhere, he resembled a haggard version of that old guy who always makes a cameo appearance in these types of stories.

"This town, it used to be different. Money didn't stand in the way of progress and truth. Now more than ever it needs somebody like him." He nodded towards the Teleporter article. "A symbol for the 'never have's'. The people who never took their chances and then they became me," he said. A dirty finger tapped onto the picture of me in that turquoise hood.

"Thanks, grandp..."

"If you'll excuse me," the old soul said and lowering his hands to his knees, began what sounded like the most painful of retching.

"Oh god," I said looking on in horror.

The old hobo hurled the contents of his booze filled stomach over the edge and into the water. After what seemed like forever and a wheezing coughing fit, he faced me again.

"People who do nothing, that's enough for evil to prevail," he gasped.

"Well, thanks for the advice." I began to part ways when he spoke again.

"Could you spare a dollar?"

You know what? Sure. Even though I'm unemployed, it could be way worse right now.

I patted myself down and reached into my back pocket. A crumpled twenty attached to some lint came out.

"Take this old timer," I said and handed him the money.

"Bless you son." He began to shuffle away.

'A symbol for the never have's,' reverberated in my ears.

"So what did you never, have?" I asked the old guy while facing nothing but the wind and an empty seafront.

"Huh?" I prompted, suddenly realising the old timer had vanished.

My boots took me further along the harbour as a wet drizzle coated me in the dank cold night. Things were quiet, almost cliché quiet. If this town really did need me then something more than an old drunk would point it out. And before I knew it something did happen.

The bass of a loud car exhaust growled towards me from a few blocks over. That heavy vibration sounded somehow familiar. Then came the screeching of tyres along with hollow crashing squeals of ripping metal. Voices raised and shouted arguments echoed into the dark. Instantly, I teleported closer to see the bright headlights staring into the rain. The car was still loudly running even without manual acceleration. I recognised a sound and it instantly struck a nerve.

In the middle of what was a pedestrian only zone lay an overturned shopping cart; bags and cans were spilled out onto the street. A shadowy lump next to the carnage began in an effort to move and get up.

"Yo! Can't you see this is the middle of the road?" The driver yelled, walking with that stoop like he didn't give a shit.

Toby Williams, son of Henry Williams, and his loud car; the scourge of my mornings.

"This is a pedestrian zone," the strained voice of the struggling man said. He then began to cough and wheeze like the hobo guy I'd just met.

"Well, dog, this damage is pretty heavy," Toby's crony the stoner guy said.

"Get back in the car Dash. I'll deal with this."

The old timer began to gather up his spilled stuff.

"Hey, are you just gonna ignore the situation? Look at my car old man." Toby reached down and spitefully grabbed the old man. We'll call him Stan for now.

"Gerroff me!"

"You going to pay for this, huh? You got anything other than this old crap?" Toby kicked a bunch of cans away.

"I just said this is a pedestrian only..." the old man wheezed.

"My family owns this damn town, old man; we can go where we like. It's scum like you that bring this place down. So how much are you going to pay me for the damages you caused?"

"Please, I have no money. I'm homeless," Stan pleaded.

"Nah, bullshit. These hobo's always have stacks man," Dash heckled from the passenger window.

"Yeah. Give me what you got. Cough up!" Toby ordered. He began to rifle through the old guy's coat.

"Please, please. I used to work for your father. What would he say right now?" Stan asked.

Okay I had seen enough, time to hero and confront this less than relevant piece of overprivileged garbage.

"Hey! Silver spoon!" I shouted.

My hands rested on my hips in my most heroic of poses. Then I teleported closer and realised that my suit was sitting on the laundry chair in my apartment. Regular Kurt stood staring at Toby Williams.

"Well look who decided to turn up. Did you leave your costume in the dryer?" Toby sneered. He had easily read my 'deer in the headlights' look and spoken like an arrogant rich boy wannabe rebel.

"You're the most cliché guy I know Toby, you know that? Rich father, dumb idiot friend, souped-up sports car, bad attitude. You're like a shitty Malfoy," I crowed. The words just flowed and he gave me a vacant look as I continued towards him.

"Well, Hogwarts is closed motherfucker!" I swung my fist out driving it into Toby's head.

"Oh shit man," Dash the stoner said, stumbling out of the car.

Yeah... 'oh shit' is right, that really hurt. Punching people isn't like anything in the movies. You would think I knew that from the bucket head incident. Adrenaline will give a guy retard strength. Okay, Turk. Just don't sell the pain and stand up strong.

"Back it up munchies or you're next," I shouted. Dash instantly back-tracked.

"Is running down hobos a new hobby?" I asked. My hands angrily working to pull Toby up. "Let me guess, your father is gonna hear about this?"

"What is this, twenty questions?" Toby failed to sound defiant.

"You're right." I pushed him away. "Get your ass outta here, this is done." My words flew towards him though gritted teeth. I took a knee to help the old guy up.

"You okay, old timer?" I asked. My arm hooked under his and I hauled him up, just as another coughing fit began.

He broke away and looked up to me with a waving motion.

"It's okay, dude. You need a glass of water or something?" I asked. He continued with this wave and then began to panic.

"What man?" Still he coughed some more, was that a lung he spit up? I stood there not knowing what he meant. Then it clicked with a thud and a crunch to my kidneys.

"Argh, urgh…" I exhaled. My body fell and I turned to see Toby standing with a baseball bat over me.

"I should… have expected… that." I groaned, bent over in pain.

"See? You've made an enemy out of me now 'disappearing boy'. Whatever beef you had with my old man was irrelevant, but since you hit me with a cheap shot…"

"God! You gonna talk me to death or what?" I asked, the pain still there.

"Now that you've got my attention…"

I rolled my eyes, but rich boy continued to lecture me. Just then a hollow metal crashing sound flew across my vision and into him. The shopping cart pushed by 'Stan' smashed and threw Toby off his feet.

"Oh, thank god for that. I thought I was going to have to actually fight him," I said and rolled over. The prominent baseball bat bruise still stinging as I got up.

"Get out of here, son. Live to fight another day," Stan said. He discarded the shopping cart and gunned towards an unarmed Toby.

"No old timer. Let me handle this." I moved to the vacant baseball bat and took hold of it.

Before I had even thought about raising my new play thing, Toby kicked up his feet and scampered away along the wet street.

"Let's roll man," Dash said.

After I'd made half a step towards them, their car doors slammed and they backed out of there fast.

"Yeah, you better run!" I watched the headlights disappear and then I lowered myself down to the ground exhaling in agony.

"Thanks kid. This town needs fellas like you, standing up, oh god…" This time the old man yacked up a projectile stream of puke straight into his shopping cart.

"I think we both know what you mean," I said. With the baseball bat as a trophy, I teleported away before the puke fumes became too much.

'This town needs, fellas like you, standing up, oh god…'

I blocked out the image of Stan puking his guts up and took in what he said. He was right. This town needed a hero like me. I began to walk with purpose and a clear view.

First, I would clean my Teleporter costume and then I'd head back out there.

Chapter 10: An overpriced entrance fee

Considering how I'd left the Drunk Poets last time, I needed to set things straight. Those people, they were the real power and no matter how much influence certain money men had on the media, it was up to the people to decide if the world needed the Teleporter.

"Spoken word night, every night?" I read from the chalk board standing in the street by the bar. "Well, I got some words," I said and headed down.

People were here again, only this time it looked way too civilised for the place. All of them were facing the stage as a guy stood rapping into the microphone.

"That figure between the white pillars,

he just supporting racists and killers." The voice on the stage rhymed out.

I breezed past the crowd and headed for the bar, Douglas stood drying a glass with his eyes watching the stage.

"Propped up by money and greed,

whilst real people are struggling to feed," the guy continued, a solitary whoop of agreement coming from somewhere near the front.

"He's not a guy who cares for our environment,

so we up here looking to vent.

Everything about him is fake like his news,

118

but still people voted for him to choose." The rapper stepped back and raised the microphone; the audience let out a reserved applause.

"Not my usual demographic, but the right message either way," Douglas said. I looked to see him nodding at me and sending a bottle of beer my way.

"Give it up for my baby brother, Jacob!" The Big L said. She took to the stage with a clipboard.

More polite applause spread around with her brother nodding.

"Thanks man, that was called White Pillars."

"Now, who have we got next?" Laura consulted her clipboard, but I had already marched for the stage. That was after I'd taken a lengthy sip of beer and so now, with my freshly laundered turquoise hood up and a baseball bat cradled over left shoulder, I stepped into the limelight.

"I wouldn't mind sharing a word or two," I said. Heads turned with the spotlight facing onto me, so I got up onto the stage and took the microphone.

"Make it quick man, we got real readings happening tonight," Laura said in my ear. Were we good? I didn't know, no time now though, people were looking at me.

"A few days back, I uh…" The microphone screeched back as I got too close.

Great start. I took a deep breath.

"Look, this deal is better if I show you and then you people show the world. Does somebody wanna record this?" I asked and looked down at the gawping faces unamused at my presence.

Guess that's a no.

"I got your back y'all," Laura's brother Jacob said. He hopped down off the stage and whipped out a cell phone.

"It's rollin' man."

From my back pocket, I pulled out a newspaper. The same newspaper where I'd read that article about me. Opening at that particular page I presented it to the people,

"I read an article in this newspaper recently. Luckily, I found a spare copy just lying around in my apartment block," I said. The audience seemed engaged and just before continuing, I got my first heckler.

"Hey, you're the asshole who stole my paper!" a loud voice barked from the back.

"You can have it back after, sir," I quickly answered.

"Fuck you!"

"How about a drink instead?"

"Sure," the man said, seemingly mollified. "But fuck you for stealing my paper!"

There came a gentle wave of laugher about the place. Maybe the comedy route could work.

"As I was saying, this newspaper asks if the world needs me, the Teleporter. It's a pretty one-sided piece of writing if you ask me. And yes, it's mostly against me. I found out down the line that this publication is funded by Bay Valley's own Henry Williams. Well, Mr Williams, I do hope this reaches you." I dropped the newspaper and brought the baseball bat forward.

"You see this? I just so happened to have taken this away from your son, Toby. That was after he'd knocked down a homeless guy in a flash car you probably paid for. I guess that answers the newspaper headline. Yes, the world needs the Teleporter and I ain't going anywhere bitch. I'm not a marketing ploy and I'm not fictional. I am the truth this town needs. If you or that silver spoon sucking son of yours wants to come and collect this baseball bat, you come and find me."

I stood there in the dead silence for what seemed like forever.

"Was it something I said?" and just as I muttered those words there came a single roaring cheer from the back.

"Yeah! About time somebody stood up to that feckin' idiot!"

Douglas had my back and he raised a tumbler toward me.

"Yeah, fuck that guy!" Shouted the man who's paper I'd stolen. People all around me were stirring and beginning to talk. I nodded to Jacob who stopped recording, but I wasn't done.

"The truth is," I said, gathering the attention of everyone again.

"I'm not some super hero. The Teleporter just did what any decent person would do. Whether that's helping a girl out who'd had her drink spiked, or picking up an elderly homeless man off the street who'd got knocked down, or even disarming an aggressive punk kid. I used to work for that man who represents everything that's wrong with this world and the country we live in. Even I couldn't see that then, but I see it now." I took a moment to breathe before pulling the microphone from its stand, and the words continued to flow.

"Henry Williams. He mirrors everything Jacob just spit into this microphone. He is everything that's wrong with this country and what is happening right now in this town, is all because of him. The gap between rich people and those without a penny; is getting bigger every day. I'm here to do what's right, it's that simple. The Teleporter stands against that bitch, Henry Williams and all of his cronies. Right now I need a drink, so thank you for letting me vent my feelings." With that said, I clipped the microphone back in and stepped off the stage.

"He's right, ya'll," Jacob said as I passed him.

"Yeah," someone from the front agreed just as more people began to chirp up.

"The Teleporter's right, damn it!" Newspaper guy shouted.

Then I stopped dead and looked back to the bar, because standing on top of it was a red-faced Douglas; oh captain, my captain.

He shouted, "Revolutions aren't begun in the boardrooms of stuffy assholes like Henry Williams," he raised a glass, "they start with the common people; normal fellas and lasses like you and me. People who drink moderately priced booze and put the world to rights in a place like this. Money isn't power. People are power! All of you are here because of that man in the hood and sunglasses, so give him the applause he deserves!"

Douglas began to compose his choir in true singalong style, only nobody joined in and he looked like that one drunk guy trying to start a sing song.

"Can you hear the people sing... Oh, for feck's sake, it's 2-for-1 cocktails when the Teleporter is here, so sing godamnit! Can you hear the people sing, singing the song..."

People cheered in mild approval before standing up. Some of them clanged glasses together in what became an oddly musical moment of pride.

"White people, damn." Laura said with exasperation. I looked back at her stepping off the stage.

"I don't get the singing either," I agreed.

"Is this what you wanted, Turk?" she quietly leaned into my ear.

"I'm not looking for recognition or applause, I'm just looking for justice. People like Henry Williams don't deserve the position they have in this world and I'm gonna take him down Laura." Some of the people around me overheard and roared in agreement.

"Well, looks like you convinced them, with help from the D-man of course. You know that bitch from across the hall is in tonight, Casey. She's talking with some guy by the bar. She's asked after you, like every day, man. You know I preferred Tara," Laura gave me that 'look' like I should know that.

"So, you are my wingman. Ah, right," I said, trying to sound more enthusiastic than I felt.

"That bitch, she's way too highly strung for you, man. She's clever too. Now Tara, she's more laid back, she's a one hand on the steering wheel type of girl," Laura explained.

"And the other hand on my gear stick?" I flinched as Laura swiped at me.

I saw Casey standing at the other end of the bar talking to some guy. Getting closer, it looked like Marcus Preston, my former boss and fellow slouch. He faced me with a smile,

"Good to see you still alive man," he said with that jolly type of smile he had, I shook his hand.

124

"Although I hardly recognise you in that get up. Sorry to hear about what happened man. Casey's filled me in on the details. Anyway, it was good to talk with you Casey, but I gotta get home to my kids. One wife alone isn't enough for crowd control, especially with my kids." Marcus nodded and began to head out. Just before he left, he added,

"Maybe I can buy you a drink some time, Kurt. We can shoot the breeze about our hatred for Williams."

"Yeah, sounds like a good night." My eyes then met the usual disapproving frown of Casey.

"Looks like you found your mojo by publicly calling out our mutual enemy. Real subtle," she said and closed her notepad.

"What were you doing with Marcus?" I asked.

"Gathering information and potential leads. It's called investigative journalism. It's going to take more than an onstage display of you calling one man a bitch to fight this."

I could sense some resentment and then she got up to leave.

"Look Casey, wait…"

"I get it Kurt. You got fired and humiliated by Williams. Anyone would be angry, and I am sorry for getting you fired. That baseball bat, you acquired it by force I guess? Going after his son isn't the way to fight this," she lectured. But she didn't know what happened down in the harbour.

"It was shitty Malfoy who used the baseball bat on me Casey," I argued.

"And you just happened to run into him?" she glared.

"He ran into me. Well, he ran into a homeless dude actually, who wouldn't stop puking. I was walking down to the harbour district and he just happened to be cruising around."

Casey stood with her arms folded. I could she didn't believe me, and after all we had been through.

"You think I went after him because of your history? You don't believe...?"

"It's not that I don't believe you, Kurt. It's just that you're a drinker first and foremost. Look, I want you to take this." She placed a small plastic gadget face down on the bar.

"If you're thinking of taking the whole teleporting gig seriously, you're gonna need it. And if talking trash in viral videos is your way of fighting, then fine, but it isn't mine. I'm gonna fight Williams how he should be fought, through traditional journalistic investigation."

Yep, she wanted to part ways, and by using long words like 'investigation' and 'traditional' I wondered if she was just trying to say we'd both changed? I'd stood at the bar many times with a talk like this and even sober it didn't digest well.

"So, we're no longer partners?" I asked.

126

"We never were Kurt. Our paths just happened to cross at the right moment. I don't need a guy like you, super power or not, treading all over a delicate investigation.

And like that, she breezed past like we had just broken up or something. I didn't know what to do other than to lower myself onto a bar stool and ask myself if she really meant those things.

Her words, they echoed in my head.

'I don't need a guy like you...'

'You're a drinker first and foremost...'

'Traditional'.

I stared at my beer until it got warm. It had remained untouched since that first long sip. The reason wasn't because of Casey's words, but by what she had left on the bar: a breathalyser.

"I think it's about time we talked, young man," Douglas said. He'd closed in on me and interrupted my trail of thoughts that had begun to crush me. Sneakily I pocketed Casey's 'gift'.

"Another beer?"

"I'm good, Douglas."

"Well, sounds like you've had it rough recently. It gets better after the few decades of shite." He poured himself another whisky and raised it in salute to me.

"I think I'm between branches for now," I grumbled.

"This whole Teleporter thing. Tell me more fella?"

I took down my hood and removed the shades.

"Holy sweet Jesus Joseph and Mary. You look like a veiny testicle," he said.

"Gee thanks, I haven't heard that one before." I complained.

"This is me now; a jobless, one time published graphic artist who can teleport after falling into a vat of chemicals."

"Okay, strike that; you look like a veiny testicle on steroids straining on the bog that birthed a child covered in haemorrhoids."

I put the hood up again.

"I'm just pissin' you about Kurtis. Job's will come and go, so will people and the books you write. You ain't the only one who ever got screwed over. The important thing about this son, is picking your ass ass up off the ground. This Williams fecker, he's a big fish that's gonna take some hook to catch, but never write off the little man and as for you, I know it's microscopic," Douglas chuckled, pirate style.

"Well, Douglas, I gotta go and probably think about looking for a job," I muttered. He patted me on the back before gripping my shoulder just strong enough to hold me back.

"That lass with the frown, she's a clever one."

"Who? Casey?" I asked, "well, we're choosing to fight our battles in different ways," I said, looking at her.

"You know she's been in here nearly every night. She's up to something, so keep an eye out. Standing up to anyone dodgy alone in this town takes balls."

"Whatever, man. She has her battles and I got mine. I'll see you on the flipside Douglas." I stepped away from my mentor's grip and headed out the door.

Was there still such a thing as investigative journalism? And wait a minute, 'I don't need a guy like you?' Don't you mean 'not anymore?' That bitch. She just lived up to her name by pretty much using me. That's how it felt, like I had been used and discarded, not a burn my clothes used, but an exploit a guy for his powers type 'used'.

Enter alcohol at this point usually. My once one and only real friend that doesn't have a difference of opinion, or a shitty little notepad and firm glare. Booze had always been my friend without fail.

I trailed off back to the apartment with my thoughts and reclined on the couch of wisdom. Soon enough I locked onto the half bottle of tequila leaning against my old TV stand.

"What are you looking at?" I demanded of it and looked away.

"Oh, you're giving me the eye? Because you think I'm gonna drink you? You think I'm not strong enough to resist the temptation of being without booze. That's it, isn't it?" And before I knew it, I had the bottle in my hand.

"I'm not strong enough," I muttered, with a crashing realisation. An epiphany seemed to be speeding towards me from those four words, then my mind flashed back, right to the moment I'd stood in the lobby of Liqui-tech. I had just teleported from the lecture theatre with Casey. Then everything fell into place, if only I'd been strong enough to teleport us, we might have escaped.

"So what? We would have got out. Then what? It would only have been a matter of time until he caught up with us..." I gripped my hair in that meltdown way you see people do. My own conscience tormenting me with the 'what if's'.

"All because I wasn't strong enough," I said, those words sounding like sweet music to my ears. Why? Because that was the realisation.

If this were my calling, I would need to be stronger at teleporting. The only way I ever knew how to get better at something was to do it over and over again. I started out by drawing shitty comics at school from scraps of paper, eventually that became a published graphic novel.

My veiny fingers squeezed on the glass bottle, then I closed my eyes and in an instant I was standing on the roof of my apartment block. Air conditioning units blew emission filled air towards me and a bunch of pigeons scurried about. That whole hero standing on a rooftop scene is way beyond what real rooftops look or smell like.

Either way I stared that bottle face to face with its shimmering liquid full of sourness that had claimed many of my nights. No more.

"I may not be strong enough all the time." In a flash I launched the bottle high up, it spun over and then over the next building before disappearing out of view.

"But I will be."

The most horrific of tyres screeching and honking of horns blared back up at me. Guess I probably shouldn't have launched the bottle that far, but as I said before, I'm no hero.

Over the orange setting sun, I stood looking out into Bay Valley. A town where Kurt Wiseman, just a normal guy, a serial high school scribbler turned onetime published graphic novelist, partial alcoholic and yoga newbie couldn't have changed shit in this world. When I put up that hood on, tied a bandanna around my face and thrown on a pair of shades, I was the Teleporter, a guy who could change everything.

Chapter 11: Briefly losing everyone in a loud nightclub

All successful people have plans, right? And those that do put 'said' plans into some kind of a list. Using the abundance of 'free' stationary I just happened to have acquired from my time at Liqui-tech, I constructed a yellow sticky note 'to-do' list. Most of my wall space had been taken up by the clutter of bookshelves and night out mementos, such as a random stop sign and several St Patricks Day stout-shaped hats. The list found itself stuck to the back of my bare apartment door.

Objective numero uno: "Face Henry Williams as the new, improved better Teleporter," I read from the top of my list. How that would come to be I just didn't know. My hope was for destiny to step in, however, I could honour the other sticky notes with writing scrawled on them.

"Become a better Teleporter, with improved strength and moves." No sweat.

And so, imagine another montage as it fades in with me wearing a sweat band and limbering up my less than athletic body. My opponent stood facing me; an old office chair padded out with an ill-fitting jumper stuffed with some pillows. I circled my new opponent and gripped its armrests. After closing my eyes, we were on the roof in an instant with just a slight tingling at the back of my throat. The teleporter muscle was about to get its biggest workout yet. My weighty-on wheels-manikin joined me in several quick-fire teleports from roof to living room to roof.

"That gets the heart pumping, but what if I were to come at you from behind?" I said and teleported to behind the chair.

"And… pulled… you… back…?" I tugged the chair back and as it began to roll towards me, I teleported to the front with a firm jab.

"Oh, yes! That works well." And my first real move was born. The *'pull n' punch'*, a manoeuvre which could also be performed in reverse.

"I should write this down," I said, scampering to the kitchen. My hands rifled through several drawers until I found a notepad.

This will be where I record my sets of move. A busy guy like me doesn't have the headspace to record every damn move I've created, and so annotations along with stick figure instructions began to fill the pages.

'The push n' trip' became my second move, created by using my obvious power of being able to appear behind someone and then reappear in front.

"Damn," I said and for a second I admired the laid-out chair with its wheels spinning in the air.

'The 'push n' punch' came next, which was completely reliant on me connecting with my target. The wide defenceless chair was an easy feat, but a face at my height in the heat of the moment, well, we'd have to see.

Every time my Teleporter muscle began to strain, I held back and retreated to my drawing desk. I even hit the yoga mat to work on my back and obvious lack of physical strength. I reasoned, if I could be stronger, my powers could do more in combat. I attached more weight to the partially battered chair.

Over the following days, I started to use teleportation in a way that enhanced my momentum and make it work for me. I could literally throw a guy, or in this case the poor chair so hard it crashed into an air con unit up on the roof.

"I'm sorry wheels, but you're the only punch bag I got," I said, sucking air. I could feel my throat muscle pulsating and slowly my breath caught up.

"Looks like he's actually putting the work in, Lou," Vinny said. He stood there next to his partner in the backdrop of another roof training session, watching me mainly wrestling a weighed down chair with books tied to it.

"Is that sweat I see? Damn! Cardiovascular isn't a word I would have ever associated with this cat," Lou said. I flung the chair their way just as they disappeared.

I could also run towards someone at a sprint and then suddenly appear dead in front of them. A move I would come to name as the *'flash spear'*. A basic run and tackle.

"How do you like me in your ugly face, Williams?" I sneered at the newspaper cut out of my nemesis I'd taped to the chair.

This time I 'flash speared' the chair whilst swinging Toby's bat and bam, it went flying.

"I'm getting stronger," I proudly noted. I wrapped my arm around the half-broken chair and teleported back down to the apartment.

Another wave of fatigue came over me and I dropped the chair and it's now only functioning wheel.

"Clean apartment," I read aloud from the coloured sticky note to-do list.

My body turned to see the cleaning fairy hadn't been in town since forever. Empty bottles lay on every surface and if I looked at them for too long a foreign feeling of almost sickness hit me.

'You're a drinker first and foremost…' the words echoed.

Bitch. Angrily I swiped the glass bottles and tins from my cable drum coffee table and stuffed them into a black sack. Most of this 'untidy' state came down to the lack of not using a perfectly functioning trash can. I decluttered and swept the apartment letting my teleportation much of the work and the mess soon vanished.

"I can be a domestic bitch if need to be," I grimly muttered.

I stood in admiration, my hand resting on the pillow attached to 'wheels', my unlikely punching bag. That creased face of Henry Williams staring at me like he didn't even know who I was.

"Oh, I'll show you who I am," I said and laid in the first jab. Left and right hitting harder and faster, my hands didn't stop punching the soft fabric.

Angrily I continued before wrapping my arms around the chair. The rooftop briefly flashed all around me, but I couldn't quite make another teleport.

"Powers fading, huh?" I asked with a strain. The heavy chair I held up with my now less painful spine buckled and down I went.

The lights went out, whilst I spooned a chair with the picture of Henry Williams taped to it.

Three loud thumps rocked through the floor brought me out of my daze.

"It's still early," I said dreamily and held my partner tighter. Muffled voices barged into my consciousness along with more thumping.

"Turk! You in there, son?"

"Huh? Big L? It's open dude," I said and rolled over.

"Damn, son. This looks like some concerning shit," Laura laughed, I hadn't even heard her come in.

"What you been drinking this time, man?" she asked.

"I… uh, nothing," I said, knowing what it looked like. My hand peeled off the now sweat plastered picture of Henry Williams that had got stuck to my own face.

"I must have passed out." I sat up and pushed wheels away.

"Tell me something I don't know, man," Laura said. She looked around and then took a seat.

"I'm sober, honest." Then I remembered, I could prove it.

"I'll prove it, girl." I teleported to the bedroom and back. In my hand I held the breathalyser Casey had given me.

"Want me to prove it?" My finger hovered over the power button and I took one hell of a deep breath.

The device bleeped several times and eventually flashed green. On the small digital display came a tick of approval.

"Sober as a priest on Sunday, hah!" I shoved the result in her face.

"I'm proud for you son but that don't change the situation right now," she said.

"There's a situation?" I asked, easing back onto the sofa.

"Your girl, she's missing. Hasn't shown up to the bar in the last few days, man." Laura explained.

"Including tonight," she added.

"So the bitch has gone AWOL? Screw her, she's probably 'journalising' somewhere. Right now," I said getting up and grasping wheels by the arm rests, "I got other things that are more important, like training to become a better Teleporter."

"This could be serious, man," Laura pointed out just before I headed up to the roof.

"It's probably not. Anyway, she didn't need my help. That's what she said. So, if you and Douglas want to be pals with her that's cool. I'm down, but right now I'm busy. We'll hang out some time," I said and flashed upstairs.

A second later I returned and caught Laura leaving.

"Her door is literally there. Give it a knock," I said.

"Whatever man, peace out," and closed the door behind her.

A sticky note broke free and danced towards me before falling at my feet.

"Be a better friend to my friends," I read.

"Ah, later." All creatives have the right to procrastinate and so before heading back up to the roof, I grabbed my yoga mat.

"Night-time roof top yoga. Is there anything more badass?" I asked myself and ignored the obvious conscious worry.

Should I be concerned that Casey had gone missing? Thoughts like these began to burn into me and were throwing me off balance. I expected Vinny and Lou to appear at any minute telling me what to do. Except they didn't.

"And breathe." I said with a full-bodied exhale. My footing slipped in distraction.

'Your girl, she's missing. Hasn't showed up to the bar in the last few days man…' Big L's words floated through my brain.

As I said Casey's door was literally across the hall from mine, so down I went. Muffled voices coursed towards me as I opened my door.

"This in an intervention yo!" The Big L said, striding down the hall . She filed in with Douglas and her little brother Jacob.

"Who in the what now?"

Somebody powered the main light on and I could see the full group emerging from the hallway.

"Don't answer his questions man, that's the rules. We tell him how we feel," Laura ordered. Behind Douglas came another familiar face, Marcus Preston my old work buddy/boss.

"We would appreciate it if you took a seat and listened up, fella," Douglas said. Even his serious face seemed comedic.

"Marcus? What are you doing here?" I asked and sat down.

"We are all here to tell you we need you, man," he said.

"Bay Valley needs you." Jacob nodded.

"Your friends need you, son. I need you." Laura was laying it on thick. Still I looked at them all in confusion.

"I need you," another voice said.

I frowned, turning towards the door. There she stood, again with that snake tattoo and innocent stare.

"Damn it Jordy, who invited you?" I demanded, charging at the door.

"Don't look at me. There's enough crazy bitches in my life," the Big L held her hands up in the air.

"Thanks Jordy, but no thanks." I guided her out the door and faced my 'intervention'.

"Look guys, I'm sober. Have been for days…"

"That's not why we are here, son," Douglas said, "now you need to listen."

Marcus cleared his throat and piped up,

"Liqui-tech made me redundant this week. They half-ass fired me. It hurts man, I'm the half-assed guy in that company."

"Shit. What happened?" I perched on the end of my couch.

"It's Casey, they saw me talking with her."

"That bitch!" I said. Damn her for getting another innocent decent hard working guy fired.

"It's not her fault, if you just feckin' listen Kurtis," Douglas grumbled.

"Look. We think Liqui-tech may have something to do with her going missing. She was supposed to meet me a couple of nights back and she didn't show. We were in the middle of something big… then nothing," Marcus admitted.

"So, we need the Teleporter to break in there and break some bones, man," Jacob said, jumping up and punching the palm of his hand with a loud slap.

"This is that moment kiddo. You wanna reel in that big fish? This may just be your opportunity," Douglas encouraged, but I had already started moving forward.

"Let me just see if my skinny jeans are dry."

The final Teleporter costume Mark Three or Four goes a little something like this; old boots half zipped and laced, check. Purple skinny jeans of the clean and dry persuasion, check. Turquoise hood up, check. Badminton knee pads used as elbow pads, check (I may need to drop a mother-fudger or two and the elbow is hard right?). Purple bandanna covering lower face, check and to finish: Funky flashing Elvis sunglasses over my eyes.

"Lose the damn shades, man," the Big L ordered. She was right, normal shades would have to do.

"Come on, man, it's night time," Jacob groaned. He was right, no shades would have to do.

Breathalyser, check. Baseball bat, check. Two miniature bottles of whisky and vodka, well, you never know, check. I stuffed all the above, apart from the bat, into my back pockets making me walk like I'd had shat myself, check.

"Here man, try this. I got a new one anyway," the Big L said. She unclipped her security grade multi tool belt.

"Keep the flashlight," she said, taking back her mace spray and cell phone.

"A utility belt. I really am a hero," I said. My hands resting heroically on my hips; finally looking as good as I ever would. Now, I have to stress Big L's size stood a tad wider than me.

"Wear it like a sash man. I know I got more junk than you son, but jeez, come here…" She pulled me in and wrapped the belt over one shoulder. It was a perfect, after she'd dressed me like the child I was. I could even wedge the baseball bat behind.

"Final costume," I declared proudly, "check."

"Now let's go and possibly save someone who's probably been kidnapped, but we aren't too sure yet."

I led our crew out. We were supposedly heading into battle and it felt good to be striding forward with some good friends by my side.

I looked to Big L and her brother, my two main people who had my back. She wore her dark security clothing with lace up dark red boots and he wore those low riding jeans and a cap. I withheld offering him a belt, after all, he did write his own rap songs. I looked over at the others who I'd considered my mentors; Douglas, the old man I would aspire to become and Marcus, a good hearted slouch-type guy who had been wronged by the same forces as me. Then you had the obsessive weird snake girl Jordy who just wouldn't go the hell away. Did she live in the building or something?

"Jordy, seriously, don't you have a home to go to?" I asked. Our power walk formation stopped just as Jacob stretched up and snapped a pic of us all.

"This Justice Crew is goin' on the 'gram'," he grinned, and whilst I threw a hard stare towards snake girl, Douglas took a swig from a metal bottle he'd concealed in his big flasher-style coat. That left Laura glaring into the distance and my former boss smiling from ear-to-ear in that jolly way.

"I was just heading out," Jordy said trying to mount a defence. "You guys heading anywhere cool?" she asked.

"You wouldn't like it. Retribution, a little corporate espionage and perhaps rescuing a damsel in distress," I told her.

"And you ain't invited!" Laura blurted. She held the lobby door and we busted out onto the street. "We goin' in my van and there ain't no space for extras."

"You wanna share with the rest of the class Douglas?" I asked. My hands reaching out towards his shiny metal bottle of goodness.

"Nay, lad. This old tin vessel is mainly for bludgeoning, son. If it gets to fisticuffs, an old boiler like me needs his equaliser." Douglas pocketed the bottle and we got into Laura's van.

"Anybody thought of a strategy or plan?" she asked.

"Uh, nope. How about we head to Liqui-tech, scope the place out. Bust in there and see what the deal is?" I suggested.

Marcus hopped into the van and instantly reclined himself into a fur covered chair by the back doors.

"Sounds like work to me. Maybe I'll hang back in the van, this chair is comfy, man," he said, "remember Casey is the priority. She's in deep with this investigation stuff," he added.

"Bust Casey out. Take Williams down. Sounds like a plan," I agreed.

"We won't have to if she's ready to move on this." Marcus winked at me and the van pulled out into the road.

"Give us some tunes, little bro!" Laura commanded.

"I'm on it, hope ya'll like Tupac!" Jacob laughed and turned the radio dial.

"Ghetto gospel. Old school," I observed.

I liked my rap classic and with a collaborative effort between genres. Douglas rolled his eyes and swigged the metal bottle, again.

"Ah, not feckin' Elton feckin' John again," he blurted.

The bus journey was normally horse shit. I swear the route took us past my apartment twice before heading north towards Liqui-tech.

A few minutes later we arrived to the beat of a gangster rap soundtrack with our driver and front passenger both bobbing to the beat.

"We here ya'll." Laura pulled up around the corner and from this vantage point we could see the shrubbery either side of the glass fronted building.

"The front doors are way too exposed for a direct approach. That could be a problem," I said.

"Around back?" Laura suggested.

"If you're consenting love," Douglas gave his best dirty old man chuckle.

"D-man, wash your damn mouth. I expect that from Turk but not you, an actual adult," Laura said.

"Can we get closer?" I asked. My hand gripping the van's door handle as it crept further along the street.

"Looks like some heavies are snooping around the lobby," Jacob said.

Sliding the door open, I squinted into Liqui-tech. Security-types seemed to be crawling all over it. Then my vision scoped out a nearby hot dog stand.

"That's new," I said and nodded my head for Laura to move further along. By now my feet were already trailing towards the aroma and it smelled good.

"Turk! What you doin', man? You gonna get seen." Laura's voice echoed toward me, but I had already gone.

"So what does a friendly neighbourhood hero gotta do to score a meal around here?" I asked the 'foreign' looking guy who smiled my way.

"Mr Teleporter, a real hero of the neighbourhood. I see your video, good fighting. Free hot dogs for life!" he beamed.

"Hot damn! I'll take that, I am unemployed after all," I said.

"They're good, trust me," came the strained voice of a man said as he emerged out of the Liqui-tech shrubbery.

"Stan?" I couldn't believe my eyes, it was the hobo from the Harbour, the guy Toby Williams had run over.

"Best meat on the street," the old soul said. I was already applying ketchup and even taking a bite before it hit me.

"Yes sir, the best mechanically recovered meat on the street," the server announced. My teeth sunk into the soft bread and the vinegary taste of ketchup hit my tongue.

In my head Vinny and Lou were standing there shaking their heads disapprovingly and saying in slow motion, 'don't eat it...'

They were right, I just hadn't put together why Stan was yakking his guts up last time. Maybe because of the booze, or the fact street meat was unsanitary. Maybe both.

"Quit fooling around man and get your ass in here!" Big L shouted and with that, I dove back into her van with hotdog in tow.

"I'll just save that for never," I said, literally wiping my tongue clean. `"Let's head around back."

The van gunned forward and dipped to the left, then another left and we were around the back of Liqui-tech. Into the service area we went, filled with dumpsters and faceless windows stretching up high. As Laura drove us forward and underneath the building out of view, none of them showed any signs of life.

"Looks like we're out of sight for now," she said. The small road sloped downwards.

"Kill the lights and engine," Douglas ordered.

"Check. Now what?" she asked.

"Now we get inside. Let me go in first and check it out. If I get close to anyone I can always teleport out of sight," I said.

"That actually sounds like a good idea. I dig, we need to find that bitch and get her out. That's priority Turk; no distractions and no hotdogs," Laura commanded.

My hand still grasping the soft bread, "I'm gonna launch this monstrosity in the trash. If I don't come back, it's probably food poisoning, so come get me,"

I said and headed out. Before I'd slid the van door open, Marcus stopped me.

"There's a fire exit just through there, man. Past those cars, it's never locked, I use it when I'm late so I don't get seen by anyone. Least back when I worked here. Shit, man," Marcus sighed.

"It's okay, man, we're gonna get some justice. This isn't just a rescue mission," I said quietly so that only Marcus could hear.

"I know. Look, I gotta make a call, see you soon." Marcus patted my shoulder and then hopped out with his cell phone.

"If you ain't back we comin' in after you dawg," Jacob called through the open window.

"You stayin' in the van bro. You going to college next year and don't need no criminal record..." My rescue mission had begun just as Laura and Jacob began to bicker.

I moved away from the van and just caught Marcus' phone conversation with who I presumed was his wife.

"Yeah. Looks like we are ready to move in on this soon. Stand by..."

Huh? That's some weird stuff to say to your wife. Maybe they ran the house like a military operation? I shrugged my shoulders and headed into the shadows underneath Liqui-tech.

A bunch of cars were sitting parked and unattended. Then I recognised the dented grill of

Toby William's classic shitty sports vehicle. The one he'd used to knock down a homeless dude.

"Mind the hobo," I said under my breath and before I knew it, my fingers had grasped the utility belt sash around me. Laura was a resourceful lady, and on this belt, she'd handily left a permanent marker.

Obviously, no graffiti efforts are ever complete without the resemblance of male genitals, and then the words I just muttered. 'Mind the hobo', only this time it was written in big bubble font across the front window. Then just for good measure, I kicked off the wing mirror. Well, he had suckered me with a baseball bat.

Moving on, I headed deeper into the underground parking lot. As sketchy as that phone conversation Marcus had been having, he was right about the open door.

"Bingo," I said and I was in. A concrete staircase went up and so did I, until I reached familiar territory of the ground level.

My eyes peered through a slit in the glass door and onto the expensive marbling that made up the Liqui-tech lobby. Two heavies stood staring out into the night through high windows. Nobody unauthorised was getting through that revolving door tonight.

Now where would Williams be keeping Casey? Probably the place I dreaded going back to most; his office where he could manipulate that tortuous inner ear ringing.

Just as I found myself tackling the stairs to his top floor lair, the bass of voices trailed back down to me.

Shit. I had to get off this staircase and do it now. In my wisdom, I decided to risk it and headed out onto the lobby floor. With the gentlest of moves and without a sound, I let the door close behind me and considered my options.

I heard voices from where I'd just come, so that was out. Up ahead the two heavies were looking out into the night. To my left was the demonstration theatre and probably yet more eyes to spot me. My only option stood directly beside me; the elevators in all their claustrophobic glory.

I had to move, nobody had seen me so far, but for how long? With my back facing the nearest elevator door, I pushed on the call button. Instantly the doors crept open, my eyes remained firmly glued on the two guys with their backs still turned away from me. My feet double-stepped backwards and over the threshold.

I took the ignorant approach in tackling my debilitating fear of being enclosed. The dry musk of plastic elevator hit me and my heart began to pound faster. Just as I scoped the button panel, I realised my ignorance had been a grave mistake, for I wasn't alone in the elevator.

"I guess you are as stupid as you look," a voice commented. Henry Williams, it had to be. Hands grabbed me spitefully and with brutal force I was thrown against the metal elevator wall.

Before I could recover they were on me.

"Grab him," Williams ordered. He glared with both shirt sleeves rolled up and his two fists primed.

His security handled me firmly and before I could resist, Williams stepped in.

"Let's go for a ride," he said and grasped my utility sash.

I saw a neon glow emanating from his left wrist and just when I braced for impact, my body unwillingly teleported.

Carpet and the breeze of air conditioning hit me as I landed. My feet stumbled beneath me whilst I crashed downwards to the floor. My internal compass spun inside me. Did we teleport? I wasn't in the driving seat.

Two shiny shoes came into view.

"Get him up!" Williams ordered.

"Nice utility belt. And the bat, I'll be taking that back." I felt the bat yanked out from my sash. Defensively I turned with a view to punch, but the room spun as I realised we were in Henry Williams office? How did I get up here so damn quick?

Toby Williams came out of nowhere and stabbed the bat forward; my stomach retched in pain. It had done enough to wind me, but I endured and charged. This time a debilitating ringing erupted in my ears. Not this again.

Somebody shoved me into a chair before my legs collapsed.

I looked up to see Henry Williams standing alongside his bat wielding son, smirking in the safe confines of their office lair. The pair of them seemed to have that half-smirk, like they had won. Maybe they had because even after all that soul searching, getting stronger by wrestling a chair called 'wheels' and even yoga, I'd still found my ass beaten and me sat on a moderately comfortable chair.

My arch nemesis held that familiar remote control with his finger primed and I got a better view of the glowing light that was strapped around his wrist. It looked like the fitness watch from hell, complete with a sloshing electric blue liquid for a screen.

"You see, Mr Wiseman, you were the ultimate Guinea pig for the technology Liqui-tech has come to harness. We don't need to pump a bunch of poison though a guy to make him like you. We just need this." He shoved the device in my face.

"Shove it up your ass, Williams," I blurted.

"Maybe you should crank up the volume a little," Toby suggested like the creepy sidekick he was. 'Screw him' I thought, 'and the bat he spun in one hand. What a little kid.'

"Sounds like a good idea, son. Then maybe this guy will remember some manners."

The ringing came again only louder and this time I concentrated hard. Just block it out and try to get out of this situation. My veiny hands gripped armrests and unwillingly I grunted and tensed.

"Fight it!" I shouted through gritted teeth.

This only seemed to amuse the bad guys whilst they toyed with me. My anger began to boil over, everything that had happened to me since the last time I was in this office, to Casey saying what she did, it all began to suffocate me. Just under the surface of every normal average man or woman is a lot of pent-up anger and frustration.

Why does the rich man control us? Why can he take it out on us and win? Sometimes anger can fuel a way out and so I shakily planted one foot in front of the other. With great difficulty, and not a lot of speed, I stood up. The persistence of the ringing tried to overpower me, but this time I was a stronger Teleporter. I took one step forward then another, it was like moving through thick clay. My fingernails buried into the flesh of my palms as both fists clenched. With all my might I swung.

Toby's ugly rich boy smirk got smacked the hell off his ugly mug, with me groaning in demon-like rage. He dropped the bat on the way down.

Escape was objective one, so I focused all my power and energy on teleporting just far enough out of the office lair. If I could just get behind the glass wall and into open plan office space.

Again, I took a stance and ignored the ringing as much as I could. Henry half-checked his downed son and then the remote he held in his hand.

Just me and him for now.

The moment footsteps closed in from outside, my hands tensed and I teleported only to have the ringing hit overdrive and pull me back.

"Hah, you're too weak. Take him down boys," Williams ordered. In the few seconds he'd taken to speak, I'd mustered up every ounce of my strength and regrouped.

"I am, the Teleporter!"

In a brilliant flash move, my body evaporated out of the bonded office and clear away from the ringing interference. Glass exploded and blew the approaching pair of security guards off their feet and onto their backs.

I opened my eyes just in time for a perfect landing outside of Williams' now exposed office. His entire tempered glass wall now sat in a thousand broken pieces. More importantly I had got out.

"What have you done? You reckless son of a bitch!" He marched wrathfully forward and onto the broken crystal strewn floor that had become like an ice rink.

My energy levels were zapped, and adrenaline alone brought me into Williams' path; he slipped and slid my way as I stumbled and found myself crashing into him. Down he slithered with me somehow managing to stay up.

"Where's Casey?" I growled and gripped his open collar. "Damn it, Williams. You tell me where she is?" I yanked on his shirt again, my anger bringing my energy levels back.

"Downstairs. She's going to be my latest test subject…"

Just when Toby ran in with a high swing I swooped down and he missed with his bat. He'd failed to realise that the floor was loose and skated forward in what was the comical move of the night. He followed through with the bat and struck a nearby cushy chair which sprung the bat backwards and towards its owner. I looked to see Toby Williams striking himself in the head. Own home run. He flopped to the floor and the bat rolled towards me.

"You're a piece of shit, Williams," I growled and picked up the bat. With my back turned, I sensed movement and teleported to the side of the room. A meathead security guy stumbled into thin air whilst I reeled back and swung.

"KABLAMO!" I shouted as wood collided into his skull.

Henry Williams charged into me and we disappeared again. In an instant, we landed back in his office with me flung forward. I stopped myself just before the huge glass desk.

"I'm just getting used to this gadget and already I am better than the Teleporter. You really are worthless…"

I jabbed the bat into Williams' chin. He instantly put a hand up to fend off the blow, so this time I went low. I gripped him with one arm and pulled, he slipped forward and clanged into his own desk. Seeing this man reduced to his knees brought me nothing but pleasure. His sweaty hands sliding over what was probably an expensive desk.

I showed no remorse and swung the bat high. With Williams in sight, I focused on my target. The hickory slammed down and past his slithering existence as he evaded harm. My momentum had given me but one option. More glass shattered into a thousand glittering pieces in what I felt was a beautiful display of rage and destruction. Hell, I even grunted and shouted like a true angry badass. What a guy.

"You ham! That was an eight grand desk," Williams screamed, sounding like that demeaning boss we've all had.

"Not anymore, now sit your ass down," I barked and pushed the bat out.

Williams fell back into the nearby chair. Furiously I pushed down on him holding the bat straight across his neck.

"I swear if you have done anything to Casey, it's your ass on the line."

He struggled and began to choke. Screw him, let him sweat.

"I didn't ask for this ability," I said and let go of my grip just as he turned blue. The chair tumbled over, and he began a pleasant coughing fit before lying still.

"Yeah, stay down, bitch."

Crunching over broken glass, I moved back out into the office area. My beating heart had just settled down when I teleported to the elevators. One fight was over, now I needed to focus on the mission.

"Phew, this is thirsty work." I said taking down my hood. I picked out a small vodka bottle from the sash.

"A sip and nothing more…" I promised myself.

My eyes turned to see Williams appear from thin air. He crashed straight into me and we went down. Vodka spilled and the baseball bat rolled. Just as it went out of reach, Williams grasped and pushed the wood on top of me.

"How do you like the feeling of a crushed windpipe?" he asked with a strained duck-like voice. His red sweaty face glaring down at me with one pulsating vein popping out.

"I've had better," I said, with a smirk.

His free hand slapped me dead across the face. Bitch! It only angered me more and so I lifted. We rolled over once and then twice. To my right I could see a water cooler; if I could just pull it down and over Williams that would work. One more roll would bring me closer. He pinned me harder to the floor and so I had to heave. My power somehow pulling through.

Then I realised, why don't I just teleport away?

I did and Williams pushed down hard onto the empty floor as I landed on my knees next to him. My hand took the mostly spilt vodka and I sucked the remnants out.

"That's' better," I said between breaths.

We both began to stand, but I was quicker and placed my hands on his back with a grip.

I charged with him in tow and my body hauled Henry Williams forward. I launched my heavy load back to his office and my hands let go. He stumbled onto broken glass and into a slowly recovering security guard; they tumbled in a pile with me wiping my hands with a job well done.

"Now really, stay down, bitch." I commanded and teleported back to the elevators.

My feet began to wobble as I landed. For a second I took to a knee and grabbed the bat. Before me the nearby elevator dinged and the doors slid open. Not more of them, not now.

"There he is," the familiar and wonderful voice of the Big L said. She pulled me up to my feet.

"Where is he?" Marcus Preston asked. I pointed towards the wreckage up ahead.

"Let me handle him. You guys go," he added and marched away.

"Come on, Turk, I left the D-man downstairs to charm his way past security," Laura said, and we shuffled into the elevator. My claustrophobic thoughts now at the very back of my mind.

The doors closed and down we went.

"Williams said something about using Casey as a test subject," I mumbled. My fatigue apparent, and then the elevator doors swung open.

"Here's my feckin' security pass," the voice of Douglas shouted.

He moved into view and swung his metal bottle up into the jaw of a security dude. Damn, the guy went down.

We blew out of the elevator and met the fighting Irishman from Boston.

"That wasn't the first fella who challenged me," he grinned back at us. Two other guys were laid out on the marble floor.

"I take it the lass wasn't up there?" he asked.

"She's going to be a test subject," Big L said behind me. I was already making a bee line for the demonstration theatre.

"Well, not if we can stop them first, sick bastards," Douglas said. The doors came into view, I had half an inclination to teleport in there, but I didn't.

My head peered around the partially open door, only to reveal a line of heavily armed guards standing in a line. On their belts were guns.

"We've got a problem," I whispered.

"Let me take a look, son," Douglas said.

"Well, feck me. He's got his own private army. I can see the lass, she's behind some glass."

I pulled Douglas back and after squinting I could make out Professor Receding Hairline and glasses combo standing beside a handcuffed Casey. She had been dressed in a type of wetsuit without anything on her feet and hands.

"We need to get in there," I murmured with frustration.

Douglas casually stepped back and took a big swig from the bottle. He then peeled off one side of his jacket and unzipped his flies.

"Drunken lout mode activated. Step aside," he ordered.

"Wait, they got guns D-man," Laura said,

"You ever see a drunkard get shot for being drunk? Plus, you need a distraction, this is my moment." And like that, Douglas stumbled into the theatre all loud and unruly.

"I wanna talk to a feckin' scientist..."

"I don't wanna look," Laura moaned, so I watched instead and somehow it worked.

The line of armoured men gradually mobbed the apparently drunken Douglas.

"Step back, sir. This is a restricted experiment."

"I'll show you me invite, hang on…" Douglas ordered.

"Sir, no liquor is allowed in here…"

"Teleport past them, man. Go." Laura said and so I moved.

Something blocked me from busting straight into the experiment area, so my teleportation skills took me as far as the stage. I stood there looking through the glass. The big entrance I'd planned had probably been denied by whatever signals the experiment gave off.

"Screw it," I said and swung the baseball bat. With a forceful stride the wood clapped against the thick glass and it bounced away loudly.

"Shit!"

The Professor and his two science cronies clocked me along with Casey. Beside her were two meatheads, but not the usual type. These two were the very same who had stood outside the Paradise nightclub. 'Bucket head' and 'Rick'.

A handcuffed Casey mouthed 'help' at me and then 'Rick' backhanded her in the mouth. Bastard, he'll pay.

A feeling of several eyes focussing on me seemed to come from somewhere. That ruckus Douglas had caused had turned silent and I spun to see a line of handguns all pointing my way.

"Don't just stand there fellas. Do what I pay you to do!" Henry Williams shouted. He emerged through the door with a gun pressed against Marcus Preston, and the Big L following with both hands up.

"Get outta here, Turk!" she shouted.

"Shut up heavy girl. I give the orders around here." Williams marched forward and pushed his two hostages down every step. Clocking that his goons hadn't moved, he said,

"Oh, for god sake, I'll do it then."

Williams kind of stumbled forward with the gun pointed towards me. Wildly he unloaded the damn clip and gunshots rocked everyone as they ducked and cowered. Me, I teleported beside him.

"You leave my friends alone!" I shouted with an emotional-adrenaline fuelled punch.

"Get him!" Williams barked before he could recover and turn on me. His armed security scrambled forward, but again I flashed away onto the stage.

The glass divide stood with several bullet holes and cracks, so I gripped the baseball bat and got ready to take another swing. Before I could move another inch, a hand clutched the bat and I heard his voice.

"This is where you lose Teleporter. And you get a front row seat to watch." A thousand hands pulled at me as my limbs were held down. They forced me to watch just as Williams teleported beside the confined Casey.

"Now let's continue with the scheduled experiment," he ordered.

"But Henry, these levels are simply too dangerous to contain. It's a surprise Wiseman survived. She certainly won't," the Professor argued.

"I pay you for results Rice, not an opinion," Williams barked. He pushed the two heavies away and grabbed Casey like a rag doll.

"No!" I shouted from my obvious entanglement.

"Get out the way you dirty fecker!" Douglas shouted from nearby.

In the corner of my eye I could see movement coming nearer and nearer.

"Out the way skinny boy," the big L shouted. She gripped the nearest guy and launched him off stage.

"Anyone else wanna go?" More challengers stepped up to her and she wrestled them away. The Big L even threw a guy into the cracked glass shattering it even more.

"Stand by Professor Rice. Begin the run up," Williams ordered. He teleported away with Casey.

I could see him high up on the platform struggling with Casey. They were between the tanks that were filled with that freaky electric blue stuff.

"Begin the run up," he repeated as Casey desperately tried to break away.

"Stay still bitch." He swiped at her with the gun.

"Running up now," Professor Rice said, just as a weight got lifted from me.

The Big L muscled my captors off me and I rolled away. My feet steadied and I got up

"Heads up!" Laura barked, and I dropped to see her launch another guy straight into the cracked glass which finally gave way creating a man-sized opening big enough for me to dive through and so I did.

"Stop him, damn it!" Williams called down.

"Rick and Bucket head. I remember you guys," I said. Without thinking and before 'Rick' could even react, I launched my foot straight up and between his legs.

"KABLAMO! In the nuts."

The first time I hit this guy dead in the nuts outside Paradise, he went down howling. So, imagine that kind of deal whilst having both of your legs amputated and being burned alive. And down he went, clutching the goods.

The other guy hesitated for a moment and I darted around him. He turned, but the metal bottle yielding Douglas swung high and wide.

"Got your back son," he said, watching the guy hit the tiled floor.

"Stop! No!" Casey pleaded. The tanks began to vibrate with a deep bass filling our ears.

My hands grasped the ladder rungs, but I knew I could get there quicker and so I did. With both feet on the metal grating I landed. The bubbling tanks of liquid turning darker as I moved.

"Just hold it, kid," Williams ordered. He pointed the gun my way and so I stopped.

"Leave Casey out of this."

"This bitch has tried to ruin me too many times. She's just a pest and what do we do with pests? We exterminate them. She could have lifted the whole lid on this thing and blown it wide open. Not today, bitch."

His slithery grip dragged her back and I saw him kick something into view.

"We're totally experimenting today." Williams laughed.

He awkwardly footed what looked like a car battery.

"What if we were to mix a battery and a prying interfering bitch together?" His foot clipped the battery and it dropped into the drink. Sparks and bubbles rose making the solution look deadlier than ever. "Now, just hold on a moment Wiseman, while I..."

"No!" I lurched towards them in a flash move of desperation.

My arms tangled with theirs. Williams laughed, and Casey shrieked. Me, I tried to grunt heroically but all my efforts fell to complete shit while we danced with potential death.

In the three-way tango, Casey came off the worst. She was thrown off the edge and ended up head first in the same tank as I had before. But this time the liquid seemed to swallow her whole.

"No, you bastard," I cried in full charge mode. My arms grasped out and Williams dropped the gun down below.

"What have you done?" I asked. My eyes turning briefly to the ever-darkening chamber.

I threw out a kick to Williams' stomach and he lurched forward. Everything slowed down. Lights above me shone and I grabbed Williams by the scruff. For a moment I took it all in. We were up high over the lights, we could have been two sports entertainers up on a cage, fighting for our lives. The only things missing were cameras, crowds and commentary. For just that split second, I lived that moment.

I dragged Williams to the ladder with everything he had ever done flashing before me. My grip on him was spiteful and sharp. We soon ran out of walkway and my body worked in autopilot mode readying this man for the ride of his life. My hands tightened and without remorse, I pushed him into thin air and clear away from the tanks. In a spectacular dive, he darted downwards.

Both Professor Rice and one his cronies scurried away as the lump of Henry Williams crashed down onto a bench full of computers and various beakers filled with chemicals. Just like the cage matches I'd watched, I stood looking over the destruction.

Everything around me then shook. The grated platform I'd been standing on wobbled and shuddered as it became unstable. A loud metal creaking sealed the fate of the Quantum Displacer and I teleported down to the ground.

I landed and glanced up to see metal vibrate and snap.

"It's become unstable," Professor Rice yelled.

"Thanks for the input Professor. I think we can see that shit storm approaching," Douglas barked. "Shut it down."

"Get back everyone," I ordered. Douglas and the Professor climbed through the broken glass and away. I stood there waiting to see what would happen, and then it did.

A bright flash killed the lights and they clunked back on as the metal platform above snapped. The right tank lurched forward to collapse and stopped just before spilling. The left the tank dropped down to the solid floor and smashed. Glass cracked and broke. A wave of bubbling blackness flowed out with a hiss. My feet were soaked, but I had already gunned for what looked like Casey.

"Casey?" I cried, with a panicked high pitch tone.

My hands gripped her partially melted wet suit and I scooped her up. The handcuffs were still intact and kept her arms together.

"Casey?"

I looked around in a panicked daze and then remembered the chemical emergency shower that stood in the corner. I darted to it and got us underneath it. My free arm pulled the lever and water rushed over the both of us. Somehow my back held up and I lowered her down as more water flowed over the melted suit.

"Casey? Come on, wake up," I said. My fingers ran through her now dark green hair. The black liquid washed off her skin, but it left a red bruised tone.

After several shakes she didn't respond.

"Shit. Casey, come on, come back to me?"

Do I give mouth to mouth? Was her heart beating? In a panic, I scooped her up again and tried to find some help.

I headed for the way out when movement caught my eye. Somehow, he had managed to survive, I guess those rich bastard types never die easily. And even though Henry Williams looked the worse for wear, he'd begun to stand up. The white shirt on him, now stained several colours of chemical, was melting and burning away. He pulled away a glass beaker that had lodged under his right eye. Blood began to trickle down his face as he swaggered out of the wreckage.

Before he could say anything, I shouted to him,

"You bastard. Look what you have done. She's dead."

As I uttered these words her body began to stir and move. In my hands Casey momentarily turned rigid; my grip couldn't handle the movement and she slipped to the now drained floor.

"Give me a goddamn gun," Williams croaked. He shifted through the shattered glass.

"I said give me a fucking gun!" he leant down and held a hand through the broken glass. With just a couple of moves he'd taken a gun and was pointing it my way.

"This is how it ends for you, Mr Teleporter. Staring down the barrel of a...

"You're right Kurt," a voice chuckled from the ground. To my surprise, Casey immediately sat up, her green hair flowing over her emotions.

"Hearing him talk, kind of makes you feel sick," she added and lurched up.

Then my room pitched into real slow-motion.

"Casey," I yelled. A bright flash filled the room; gunfire.

The world paused for a moment as I saw Henry Williams aiming into the gut of Casey.

NO!

I turned my neck, and my world collided with my fictional past. I saw Lou cradling a blood covered Vinny. Not these guys, not now. Vinny had got shot bad and didn't have long. He would die in his partners arms tonight. But that wasn't how 'one night' was written. That was why one night happened, because all this time you were thinking they were a double act. The twist is, Lou was just getting revenge for losing his friend and he was the only one who could see Vinny, apart from me.

Then real life came off pause and the twist became apparent.

Casey stood dead still after Williams fired and I fell back and down to the floor in fear. But she didn't move, not at all. I looked up to her green wet hair resting over her partially melted wet suit.

"Huh?"

Another flash filled the room and this time Casey shunted back on one foot. Again, she stayed upright. Her arms began to rise and when they reached overhead, Casey pulled the handcuffs until they snapped.

"What? This bitch doesn't die?" Williams screamed. He moved the gun up to Casey's face, but she had already stepped in.

Her hand swiped the gun away and then she put the other hand around Williams' neck.

"Call me a bitch again," she encouraged, calmly and coldly.

"You... bitch..." she was choking him out as his feet swung off the ground. Again, his face started to turn blue.

"Holy shit," I said, coming to a realisation.

"Do, something," he wheezed pleadingly towards the glass and his goons. "Fuckin... shoot the... bitch."

Casey broke the grip.

"Get behind me, Kurt," she ordered, and I did what she said.

"Fuckin' … do it!" Williams cried, as he kicked himself away.

It started with just two or three shots, then I closed my eyes as more bullets smashed through the glass and towards us.

"We're gonna die," I screamed in full pussy mode.

"But not today we're not, Kurt. Follow me," she ordered and began to move into the enemy fire. My screams continued like the hero I was, only masked by the sound of bullets dropping to the floor all around us.

Casey bent down and I lowered with her. She grasped Williams' gun and made the biggest statement she could. She fired up high and then pointed it down at Williams.

Instantly the enemy fire stopped.

"Call me a bitch again?" she asked, glaring at her target.

"Bitch," he strained.

"That's 'bullet proof bitch' to you," she shouted and pulled the trigger. A bullet struck Williams' leg and he rolled over howling in pain.

"That's badass," I said, realising we were in control.

"Somehow, I don't think so…" Toby Williams charged with baseball bat in hand.

He swung the gun out of Casey's grip and she stood stunned for a moment.

"Oh, fuck off loser," she sneered and stepped in for a kick. Nut bag city.

He dropped the bat just in time for me to step in and hit another fatal nut shot; taking all the glory.

"KA-DOUBLE-BLAMO!" I yelled as Toby succumbed to his knees. "Now that's team work," I crowed.

Just when we were about to announce victory another intruder came to the party.

"I've had it with this shit."

'Rick' the guy who I had kicked twice in the nuts before stumbled through the mostly bullet destroyed glass. He limped towards Casey and tried to hold a gun up. She clocked him and yep, you guessed it, she launched her leg straight up and between his legs. I'm not exaggerating when I say he instantly passed out after a high-pitched exhale in tribute of a dying animal.

In the commotion I took the opportunity to grab a gun and point it at the slowly crawling away Henry Williams.

"Not so fast asshole." I said.

He turned and his image fizzled away for just a second.

"Damn it," he roared and thumped the wrist gadget that had begun leaking glowing liquid.

172

"Look at the damage you have done. You, you low earning peasant scumbags."

"You can't call me names, douche bag. I got the gun." I told him. And for the first time in my life, I fired a gun straight up into the air and into the glass screen. The noise made me jump out my skin and even whimper a little, but then the entire screen dropped in furious destruction. Again, I flinched and nearly jumped into Casey's arms.

"Question is, what do we do until the authorities show?" she asked.

"Authorities? I am the authorities," Williams smirked. He tried to get up and that was when Marcus Preston breezed in.

"For some reason, I don't think so Henry," he said.

"Preston, you idiot. What do you want?"

"To tell you that we have recorded everything." Marcus pulled his shirt open to reveal a series of wires and gadgetry.

"He's got a bomb?" I turned and asked Casey.

"No, stupid. He's an informant for the FBI."

"FBI? What?" I stood, shocked.

"And the Board of Directors. You see Henry, let me help you up here." Marcus pulled the bloodied and chemical stained guy up.

"I'm going to be getting my old job back. Well, especially as you're about to have your assets frozen. You'll have no choice but to sell your majority of Liqui-tech shares to the guy you embezzled them from in the first place. Why? Because that's what happens when you get incarcerated," Marcus explained. He shoved Williams forward and onto the stage.

"Incarcerated? Me? What for?"

"Let me see... False imprisonment, for one. The attempted murder of Casey. And of course, the various financial crimes you have committed when bleeding this company dry..."

"I have the best damn lawyers in the country. You can't touch me..."

As Williams stood defiant, we all watched a mass of incoming bullet proof vests bursting through the doors. Suddenly there were guns everywhere and shouting, lots more shouting.

"Nobody move! Police, get down now!"

I spun to see a troop of agents emerging from behind me. A badge was pushed into my face just as I realised the smoking gun was still in my hand. I couldn't drop it quickly enough and then they shoved me to the floor.

"But, I'm the good, guy," I pleaded.

* * * *

The funny thing is, it turns out the Teleporter was just a minor sub-plot in what became one of the biggest criminal busts in Bay Valley history, if not the country. All of which happened right under my nose.

I got out of there in one piece by the way. That was in case you were asking. After some initial confusion the FED's identified me as a 'good guy'. Hell, they even offered me medical attention.

Henry Williams and his private security instantly surrendered, that was after the Big L had softened them up. It turned out Williams had gotten deep into the criminal underworld and so had a lot of other Liqui-tech folks. From illegal scientific practices all the way to every type of finance crime you can think of. They stripped the building that night. Even the damn IRS showed up.

Being taken out of that place became a blur, even in the sober state I was in. The place eventually calmed down and I found myself lost amongst the flashing lights of ambulances and police cars. Every so often there would be another commotion as an arrested Liqui-tech employee passed through.

"You can't charge me for shit, you assholes..." Professor Receding Hairline/Rice was next. I watched a couple of agents drag him away as I sat on the bumper of a nearby ambulance.

This was a whole new world to me. Had I won? I guessed so, but it didn't feel victorious right then.

"How you doin' fella?" Douglas asked. He took off a blanket given to him by medic and placed it over me.

"I guess we won." I said unemotionally.

"Fuckin' A we did. Want a swig?" he asked and popped the top off his metal bludgeoning thirty-year old scotch.

"I'm not feeling it currently. Is Casey gonna be okay?"

"I think being bulletproof means she's gonna be all good man," the Big L said, pointing to Casey who was also draped in a blanket. She was talking with a pair of agents and Marcus Preston.

For a while I just stared at her, did I like her? Did her super powers change anything. Bullet proof bitch was a great name.

Then her eyes met mine. She smiled and after briefly looking at the two suited agents, she waved me over.

"Hey, Teleporter, come here," she said and in that instant, I was there.

"Agents, this is the legendary Teleporter." I nodded to their blank expressions and they nodded back.

"I can't say that we endorse any type of vigilante activity, but you were the vessel that blew Williams' crime empire wide open. Good work, all three of you." And like that they breezed away.

"So, what happens now?" I asked Marcus.

"I have work to avoid doing. I'm thinking changing the company name back to what it was before; Liqui-Med, Medical Science Research. Maybe not though, I'll think about it. I expect to see you here Monday morning or early afternoon, I want you both to be my new Brand Outreach duo," Marcus said.

"So, you get to take control of this place? Cool man." I grinned.

"Yep, back in the boardroom for the first time in years. It's daunting for a layabout like me. I'm thinking early finishes on Mondays and Fridays."

"Sounds good, Marcus. We'll see you Monday afternoon maybe," I said and nodded to the guy as he walked away.

"That's the spirit," he said with that jolly smile.

So, it was just me and a red skinned, green haired girl in a partially melted wet suit. We stood there for what seemed like forever.

"So…" she said. "Thank you, for putting in the save in there, Kurt."

"No sweat. I didn't do much other than some light brawling."

More silence came and it began to get awkward.

"So…" I said.

Is this where we kissed? That's what happens in these stories, right?

I leant in and she followed. Our lips touched and my eyes closed. A sour warmth hit me hard and immediately I repulsively pulled away and so did she.

"I guess that's out then," she said and then we both smiled.

"Just partners?"

I shook the hand she offered.

"Just partners," I agreed and we trailed off towards Big L and Douglas.

"I don't know about you guys and gals, but I need a feckin' drink," Douglas said.

"You drank literally the whole time we were here D-man!" the Big L laughed.

"I mean a real drink."

We partied and karaoke'd the evening away down in the Poetry Bar before remembering that Big L's brother, Jacob, had been left behind. He'll forgive us one day. There were pre-drinks, shots, more shots, too much beer and a sketchy late night snack made up mainly of grease.

In between, friendships were forged and reinforced. Bad guys got theirs and ultimately justice was kind of done. Nobody died, which is actually a record for these types of stories, well, probably anyway.

Either way, that cool little basement bar always seemed to be busy now. Whether that was people coming in to see me, or just to vent with words in front of a microphone.

And so our tale takes its final steps. It's early evening and the sun is shining down into the busy Drunk Poets Society.

"What are you havin' Kurtis?" Douglas asked as I sat on a bar stool, waiting semi-nervously.

"Nothing for me tonight Douglas, I've got a date." I said proudly.

"Who's the unfortunate soul?"

"Me," the smiling Tara said as she came our way. This time way less drunk or spiked. She looked nice with her long brown hair and respectable clothes; not even slightly covered in puke.

"And I brought a friend and her hubby!" Tara screamed in delight as, was that Stacey? Scurried in the door and towards me.

"It's the Teleporter, yay! Shots!" she wrapped her arms around me.

"Hey, you," I said, afraid of getting her name wrong. "Guess it's shots then," I smiled.

"Now, Turk-Wise, I want you to meet a very special man. My husband Steve," Stacey said and turned.

"Where is he?" I asked looking all round for this jock asshole.

"Down here," Stacey said.

What came next came was a genuine shock. She presented me with a hairy hermit-type of a guy. Now don't get me wrong, I have no beef with hairy hermit-types, but Jesus this was unexpected.

That's not your husband, don't be shitting me. Then they kissed and I almost threw up in my mouth.

"Hi, my names Steve. You're the Teleporter, right? Good work with taking Henry Williams down. He's a kick in the nuts to all scientists, including me."

"So you're into science?" I asked. Anyone in that field instantly became suspicious to me.

"Yeah, fusion research. This is my start-up 'SAFC'," Steve the hermit said and pointed to a crest on his breast pocket. He then pushed his sliding glasses back up his nose.

'Well, I shall have to keep my eye on you, Steve. If that is your real name.' I thought to myself.

"Well, here's to science. And fighting crime... sometimes," is what I really said, and raised a shot glass.

Across the bar I nodded to Casey. She nodded back and continued to read her newspaper.

"So, I read your graphic novel, Mr Wiseman," Stacey said.

"You like?" I asked.

"I loved it..."

'Well, leave a damn review then', is what I would have said, but instead I smiled politely.

"Especially the cool twist at the end. What's next for Kurt Wiseman?" she asked.

"I'm thinking a Super Hero comedy," I said with a wink and raised my shot glass.

Chapter 12: Someone who just won't leave

And before this story comes to an actual close, we must go back to the initial scene of our hero standing there atop of a building looking over Bay Valley. A stern breeze enthusiastically blowing by.

"Jesus Kurt, what did you eat?" Casey asked. She was foolishly stood downwind.

Or shall I say the Bullet Proof Bitch. Her green hair dancing in the breeze and resting on her brand new dark red wetsuit. It kind of matched her stained skin tone.

"It is taco Tuesday," I said.

"What about Smash Mouth, All Star?" I countered, referring to our constant discussion of what exactly our hero theme song should be.

"Way too cliché." Chopped down again.

"Broken Wings, Mr. Mister?" I suggested.

"Uh, what century are we living in?" Casey asked, and before I could say another word she chimed in.

"And don't even suggest Nickelback..."

"Damn it. Why all the hate? I like my rock middle of the road and sometimes generic," I said and looked over to see the Liqui-Med roof access door opening.

Marcus Preston in his brand new tailored suit strode towards us. His face demonstrating serious concern, looked over to me.

"What's up, homies?" he asked with a partial moonwalk, then reverted back to business mode.

"Looks like the aftermath of Henry Williams' empire is becoming apparent. This town is for the taking and now we've got our next assignment," he said.

"Another crime lord rich dude?" the bitch asked.

"Nope. A couple of small-time thugs who see themselves as 'antiheroes'," Marcus told her.

"Sounds like a walk in the park compared to our old friend Henry. So where do they hang out?" I asked.

Marcus showed me the picture of a bar on his cell phone screen. "Local talent. First shots are on me. Time to move out," I said.

"They go by the name of Ordinary and the Fall Guy. They could be tricky to bring down. Either way Liqui-Med have got your backs." Marcus stood proudly and watched as we were about to move out. Casey strode my way and I gripped her hand.

"Be careful guys."

"Don't worry, Commissioner, I, uh, mean Marcus." *"Only shooting stars break the mould."* I sang, looking past him at my partner.

"Oh, really?" Casey protested.

"Now let's take these broken wings..."

"Seriously Kurt..."

Then we did what only we knew how to do whilst still arguing. The Teleporter and The Bullet Proof Bitch disappeared into the next story.

The End. (Seriously that's it).

Authors Note

I set out to create this story with one goal in mind, which was above all, to make people laugh. Whether you as the reader did, is neither here nor there, because individually we all take different things from stories.

Under the surface of The Teleporter, there are a lot of real life themes and issues represented, which are in no way a joke of any kind, but with the wonder of storytelling it allows me to present real issues and how this book treats them.

You may have found the power hungry, villainous Henry Williams to be perceived as someone very similar to a particularly controversial well-known world leader, then again, you may not have. In my writing I have created this character and his various traits, but it's you and your imagination which did the rest. As a writer, I can only tell you what is there, but it is what you embrace as the reader and is most important, is what wasn't there. What we make up ourselves gets us through most books.

We live in an age where everyone has a right to their voice being heard, and the obvious political undertone in this book deserves to be heard too. All of our voices, as a collective, have never been so powerful in bringing change for the better in a world still figuring itself out. Even if this story has no particular morale, it contains plenty of messages.

Much like how the success of this book is decided by people, so is politics, society and change.

Kurt Wiseman is indeed conflicted with his many faults, but he is also a person who knows what to stand up for. His story is in fact a lesson for life. Enjoy it, use moderation where necessary and look after yourself. Most of all, don't abuse power because eventually it fades, for everyone. Just like Lou and Vinny would constantly remind him; look in the mirror every now and then.

I wanted to write this story a few years ago, just before deciding to draft Open Evening, but the tale needed to spend a few years sitting around in my imagination to grow. The origins of the Teleporter go back even further to series of animations I created in my mid-teens, they will never see the light of day though.

I've enjoyed the change of creating a story that is a little lighter than the usual stuff I currently have published, because we all need to laugh every now and then, including me. As I said, this is why I wrote this, because to me laughter may be the most organic natural thing we do. Having said that, I went into this project not knowing if anyone would enjoy it at all. And that may actually be the greatest thrill I ever get from writing, the not knowing or the not really being sure.

Uncertainty can be a wonderful driving force and in order for us to work and create good things, we have to be out of our comfort zone.

I must take this opportunity to thank you for reading the Teleporter and please tell me what you thought by leaving a review.

Open Evening
Lee Hall

Sometimes you don't get to choose where you are placed in the collective ecosystem of a high school.

Luke Hartford spends his days on the fringes of social inadequacy. A normal day at his small down American High School can be described as horrific. That is until events take a turn for the worse. After a vision, Luke realises there is something other than the horror of trying to fit in lurking just under the surface.

A mysterious stranger arrives in town and the teachers are acting weirder than normal. Soon enough Luke and an unlikely team of allies must fight their way towards survival, even if they don't really know who to trust. The question is, who will survive the Open Evening?

"If I can see you, they can see you."

"Amazing book that snowballs into a world of mystery and excitement..."
'Take a chance on a great debut novel...'
'Entertaining, engaging; a real page turner.'

Available now to download and in paperback.
https://www.amazon.com/dp/B01M07N4SA

Darke Blood

Lee Hall

"There are more than shadows lurking in the darkness of those trees."

Blake Malone is in search of a new start and arrives in the remote forest town of Darke Heath. The memory of his past mysteriously becomes a blur as he discovers this place isn't what it seems.

Malone shares a romantic encounter with a woman named Caitlyn and she reveals herself to be a 'creature of the night'. He learns of her story which intertwines with the history of the 'Heath'. Together they must face the evil forces of vampirism and witchcraft that await them in the Darke forest.

But just who is Blake Malone? That's something even he must fight to discover. Because 'you've never known true darkness...'

'Fascinating book that is guaranteed to produce shivers, chills and a lot of entertainment.'

'The world of vampires may seem a common theme nowadays but this book offers new territory within that world.'

'Another great read by an amazing up and coming author.'

Available now to download and in paperback.
https://www.amazon.com/dp/B072LPNX3P

Cemetery House
Lee Hall

Survival was only the beginning...

High school was only the beginning...

Haddington was only the beginning...

Open Evening was only the beginning...

The anticipated sequel to Open Evening arrives Halloween 2018...

Printed in Great Britain
by Amazon